THE CONSOLATION OF PHILOSOPHY
& Other Tales

THE CONSOLATION OF PHILOSOPHY & Other Tales

Including "The Fairies"
by Ludwig Tieck;
Translated by Bruce Donehower

Bruce Donehower

Copyright © 2006 by Bruce Donehower.

Cover Art: *Red Bear Hears the News of Bodhidharma* by Marion Donehower, 2006

Library of Congress Control Number: 2006903823
ISBN: Hardcover   1-4257-1411-0
              Softcover   1-4257-1410-2

All rights reserved. No part of this book may be reproduced or transmitted in any form or by any means, electronic or mechanical, including photocopying, recording, or by any information storage and retrieval system, without permission in writing from the copyright owner.

This is a work of fiction. Names, characters, places and incidents either are the product of the author's imagination or are used fictitiously, and any resemblance to any actual persons, living or dead, events, or locales is entirely coincidental.

This book was printed in the United States of America.

To order additional copies of this book, contact:
Xlibris Corporation
1-888-795-4274
www.Xlibris.com
Orders@Xlibris.com
33889

CONTENTS

Alonzo Petra 9

The Tale of the Shining Princess 43

The Consolation of Philosophy 58

"The Fairies" by Ludwig Tieck
    Translated by Bruce Donehower 81

This book is for Marion.

"Der wahre Leser muss der erweiterte Autor sein."

ALONZO PETRA

One

The bees were abuzz under lilac when the stranger came limping down the lane. Alonzo saw him from afar, a sailor with a garland of vinca round his neck. One shoe off and one shoe on, he came raising clouds of dust on the road that eased by Grandma's farm.

His clothes told tales of woe. Threadbare and loose to a lazy breeze, the brass-buttoned uniform drooped from the stranger's limbs like sails from a storm-chewed yardarm. The man hummed as he walked, a soft easterly smile upon his lips, and his eyes, blue as south sea harbors, stared not at the road but at the sky.

Alonzo hid in the lilac and listened. The sailor hummed a song that Alonzo knew quite well. It was one of those songs from Grandma's player piano. Unlike that old piano, he was in tune.

Sing Ho! A roving I must go!
Sing Ho! A boundless sea!
I'll sail the world fair twice around
All for love of thee!

The sailor stopped at the lilac where Alonzo hid, and he sniffed the sweet, purple blossoms. The sound of bees abuzz under lilac was louder than Alonzo had ever heard it before. The sailor—was he young, or old, or old-young?—smiled. Alonzo noticed that the sailor had burrs and meadow grass and daisies in his straw-colored hair. He noticed how a dried clot of seaweed clung to the sailor's shoeless foot.

The sailor smiled at the cloudless sky then gave his shoulders a shake, as horses will.

"How many miles to the Petra farm? Gus Petra, do you know him? I've come a powerful way to see old Gus."

Gus Petra, as anyone in the county knew quite well, was Alonzo's grandpa, Gramps. But Gramps no longer lived at the Petra farm. The angels had fetched him off to heaven, and Grandma kept the farm alone.

This news brought a wrinkle to the stranger's road-weary brow.

"Gone? Well, that's the way of it. Always arriving, never on time! Are you the grandson? Good enough. Then you shall have it!"

The sailor reached in his pocket and took out a copper coin. He thrust it through the lilac and into Alonzo's startled, sweaty hand. The coin was warm.

"Cause of trouble—nothing but! Take it. And am I sorry I ever saw it! Jackie Blackmon's the name, and I am not a thief! Only meant to borrow, never steal, and that's the live-long truth of it. Your gramps always said this coin was lucky. Lord knows I needed luck! Well, that's the way of it—one man's luck, another man's misfortune. Take it, and my apologies! Cause of trouble, nothing but."

The sailor brushed his dirty uniform and gave Alonzo a smart, nautical salute. "Hail and farewell and fair voyaging! I've a long trek ahead of me to Ma Nightsweet's Eider Hall. Don't lose that coin, I tell you. It's a charmer!"

Saluting smartly again, the sailor pivoted and headed back down the lane.

Alonzo watched until the man was out of view; then he burst from the lilac at a run.

Dr. Sugar the cow vet and Grandma Petra were in the barn injecting calves when Alonzo came in flying with the news. Standing with her broad hands upon her hips, Alonzo's grandma listened to the boy's breathless tale while Dr. Sugar repacked his long syringe.

"Hmm," said Dr. Sugar, "not every day you meet a sailor five-hundred miles from the sea."

"Show me the coin," said Grandma sternly.

Alonzo did. To his surprise, Grandma Petra had seen it before.

"Why, that coin belonged to Gramps! It's his old lucky charm. He got it 'fore we were married. See there, on the back, look what it says!"

"Liz and Gus," read Dr. Sugar.

"Ain't that a wonder!" marveled Grandma. "Gramps always said if it weren't for that coin we'd have never got hitched. How I do recall the day he lost it!

Why, he carried on like kingdom come. Who'd you say it's from? Not Jackie Blackmon, that's a mistake. Jackie did work for us back when Gramps had sheep, then he upped and joined the Navy. Poor Jack, he got himself sunk."

"Let's see that lucky charm," said Dr. Sugar, holding out his barn-soiled, medical hand. He sniffed the coin, raised one gray eyebrow, and winked. "Think it's still got some magic in it, Liz?"

Grandma frowned. She gave Dr. Sugar a friendly nudge. "You charmer, give that coin here. Alonzo, you may keep it. Wherever it did come from, it's yours by right of inheritance, I suppose. Run along now and feed that pesky mutt. He's been barking half the morning till I'm about fit to go deaf."

"See ya t'morrow, slugger," said Dr. Sugar, who knew more about saints and baseball than any man alive.

Boots, Alonzo's wiry black-haired mutt, barked excitedly when the boy came by. He wagged his tail and licked as Alonzo showed him the lucky coin.

"Down, boy, down," said Alonzo. "Be careful! See this coin? It was Gramps'! Grandma said so. It's good luck!"

Respectfully, the good dog paid some mind. He sniffed the precious relic.

Across the barnyard, Alonzo saw Grandma bid good-bye to Dr. Sugar. The cow vet, polite as ever, tipped his hat. Boots whined and growled.

"Finish your chores, Alonzo," Grandma shouted. "It's time! Time!"

With a groan and a rattle, Dr. Sugar's blue Impala rolled down the gravelly lane. Its broad, fat whitewalls raised clouds of dust.

Maybe he'll see the sailor, thought Alonzo, and he hurried off to do as Grandma said.

Two

"Lay down, I'll tell you a story."

Alonzo snuggled his head into the plump, eider down pillow, pulled the stiff linen sheet to his chin, and gazed up into his grandmother's sturdy, wrinkled face. So many wrinkles, like the lines of an ancient map. He knew already from her lavender-scented hands that the story must be about Gramps.

"Once upon a time when Gramps was young . . ." Grandma started.

"How young, Grandma? As young as me?"

"Not so young, but not grown up," she told him.

Boots the mongrel stirred at the foot of Alonzo's bed. His ears perked up, hearing what human friends could not. He whined.

"Hush, Boots," said Grandma Petra. "Settle your hash."

"Grandma, did Gramps have a dog?"

Grandma brushed aside a strand of silvery hair. "Kept it for hunting," she nodded.

"Is Boots a hunter?"

"Boots?" scowled Grandma. "Boots's a mutt."

Grandma folded her hands in her lap, composing her remembrance, ignoring Boots, who wagged.

She told the tale.

"Once upon a time, when Gramps was young, his father told him to fetch a broody hen to the farmer across the stream. Gramps put the broody hen in a sack and started off. It was getting toward the twilight time of day. Now normally Gramps could skip there and back in the time it takes a sow to have her feed. That day, it took him longer.

"Gramps went across the pasture where the hay was still in shocks. He was barefoot, and the stubble pricked his feet. He had that broody hen in burlap and he wasn't paying much mind, because, you see, *it was his birthday*."

Alonzo, who knew the story well, snuggled tight with anticipation. His room had darkened to a solemn hush of gray. Grandma kept her hands peacefully folded, and her voice went low, like it did in church. Outside, the crickets chirped.

"And so, as he thought about his birthday, Gramps came to the rickety bridge. And though he meant to cross it, instead he stood there dreaming, and he thought: *I'll just throw in a stick and pretend it's a ship and then, by golly, I'll sink it!*

"And so he did. But lo and behold what should happen next . . ."

"I know," said Alonzo, eager to repeat the oft-told tale. "A man appeared . . . No, no, not a man, an *angel!*"

Grandma frowned. She did not like interruptions.

"Not an angel," said Alonzo. "I mean a *troll!*"

"It was an ordinary ragman," Grandma said. "Lord knows we had enough."

"And the ragman said . . ."

Sonny, what's in your sack?

"And Gramps said . . ."

A broody hen for the farmer across the stream.

"*Give it to me!*" growled the ragman.

Knowing what would happen, Alonzo made a face. He mimicked Gramps' reply to the evil ragman:

> *Not for a nickel,*
> *Not for a dime,*
> *Not for the ladies of the Argentine!*

"But," said Grandma, "that greedy ragman would not take no for an answer." And she changed her voice to mimic that evil fiend.

*Trip trap, trip trap,
I'll eat you for dinner,
You scaredy cat!*

"Was Gramps afraid?" she asked him.

"No!"

Alonzo answered so forcefully that the old box-spring mattress made a noise. *Kachunka chunk. Kachunka chunk.* Boots cocked his mongrel head, and Grandma smiled, pleased that her tale was well received.

"So Gramps and the ragman tussled—to and fro, to and fro on the rickety bridge. That ragman, he was strong, but Gramps, he was a scrapper. And, just as he grew weary, the sun did set. *Uncle!* cried the ragman. He was *through!*"

Now came the part of the tale that Alonzo loved best. Grandma knew he loved it. She raised her voice to a suitable trembling pitch.

Please, said the ragman, I'm dyin' fit to starve! Uncle! Please! Have mercy! I've wives and thirteen young ones home to feed! They'll die without that hen! I promise not to cheat. Here is the very best present a lad on his birthday ever had!

"Gramps looked at the ragman, all huddled and scared. Like a skeleton, he was—all skin and bones. Gramps remembered his father's instructions: he knew he should keep the hen. But that ragman, ah, he was a charmer! He showed Gramps the present in his hand."

"What was it, Grandma?" Alonzo asked.

"You know well enough, or ought to," Grandma frowned. "Lies, sweet flatteries, and a plain Spanish copper coined for love."

"Did Gramps take it?"

"You know he did. And lost that hen, I'll tell you. More's the pity."

"Was his father mad? Did Gramps get his wish?"

"Yes—why, yes, he did. In a manner of speaking. Gramps wished on that ragman's lucky coin, and his wish come true—not all at once, but by and by, as wishes will. If it hadn't, *would you be here, Alonzo?*"

Would I? thought the boy.

"Good night, Sweet Prince," said Grandma, yawning.

The creaky old door to his bedroom swung shut and latched. Alonzo lay with his eyes wide open, staring at the shadows on the walls.

An hour went by. Maybe two. Maybe three. Alonzo knew from the plumbing that his grandma had gone to bed.

The full moon rose high enough to peep through Alonzo's open window. Impatient moon.

Boots was just as bad. He cocked his head.

"Time, time," chirped a cricket beneath the bed.

Boots, who loved to chase bugs, leaped down to do his duty, but the wily cricket vanished in a crack. Boots whined and fretted until Alonzo had no choice but to get up.

"Come," said the moon, in her willow whispery voice.

Alonzo listened. Reaching beneath his pillow, he found the lucky coin that had been Gramps'.

"This way!" chirped the cricket, and with a single bound it leaped from its hiding place, out the bedroom window, and into the warm spring night.

Alonzo took the coin and came along.

Three

On the rickety moonlit bridge, Gramps stood waiting. Alonzo came with Boots across the meadow, and Gramps saw them from afar. Gramps waited until they were close before he waved. "Evening, Alonzo," he muttered. "Glad to see you out." But his voice did not sound glad, it sounded *old*.

Gramps stood with his arms akimbo, still dressed in his red plaid shirt, the one with faded patches on the sleeves. He wore his bibs and barnyard boots, ready as always to put in a good day's work. The only thing missing was his pipe—his ratty stinkpot, Grandma called it. Perhaps he'd left his stinkpot some place else.

Gramps looked as though he could use a good night's sleep. Mud on his pants, mud on his shirt, and his barnyard boots were caked. Grandma would never have let him into the kitchen looking like that. No one trod her floors with dirty soles.

"Up kinda late, ain't you, Alonzo? Boy your age, what would Grandma say to that?"

Alonzo blushed. He knew it was wrong to roam when Grandma slept, but he did have his reasons, after all. He reached in his pocket to find the ragman's coin, and he laid it, warmed from his own body, in Gramps' dark rooty hand.

"Frogs and fritters," Gramps exclaimed, "if that ain't my lucky charm! Great Moses in the bullrushers, where'd you get it? I thought I'd never see the thing again."

Alonzo felt pleased to see Gramps happy. These days it wasn't often the old man grinned.

Gramps sniffed the lucky charm. "Yep," he said, "it's the real McCoy. Look there, Alonzo, the date—that's the year I married Liz. This side was blank; I had it etched. The jeweler, Simon Gobbler, did the work. Coined for love, and that's the truth of it. See what it says there? *Gus and Liz!*"

Alonzo nodded. Proud. He knew what the old coin had to say. More than messages, he asked: "Is it worth a lot?"

The old man stared. "Worth a lot? Great Moses in the bullrushers! Do you mean *precious*? Boy, you ain't got half the tale. *Precious!*—you'd better believe it! Or would have been, I guess . . ."

Suddenly, the old man's interest died away. His shoulders sagged, and his gnarled hand curled into a fist.

"Precious? Sure it's precious. Now it's precious *all too late!*" Gramps' voice went low, changeless in its tone as the quiet flowing water of the stream. "All those years searching, and now I've got it back. Too late, I got the coin too late! Dang blast that cheating ragman! Not my fault his coin done disappeared. Holes in the pockets day and night, a thing slips out."

Alonzo stared past the coin and into the slow-moving, moonlit stream, hearing the sigh and rush of his grandfather's words. A fishing boat floated free from under the bridge. That fisher was indeed a mighty paddler. He stopped his craft and helloed.

"Excuse me; do you know the way to sea?"

Alonzo did not, but Gramps, who had lived longer in that country, offered his two cents.

"You'll not strike sea in that!"

"Not the sea, thank you kindly," said the boatman, "a river will do just fine."

"All streams find their rivers in the end," snapped Gramps, forever short. "Instead of jabbering, you should paddle."

"Thank you," said the boatman. "Need a lift?"

Alonzo looked at Gramps, sheer as gossamer in the moonlight. His face was weathered as a mountain's northern slope. His eyes were sad as boots.

"Well?" said the boatman, smiling.

Gramps scrunched his brow as he always did when he was mad.

"Nothing I'd like better than to get off this dang-blasted rickety bridge!"

"Well," said the boatman, "why don't ya?"

Instead of answering, Gramps began to pace. To and fro, to and fro—that old bridge shook from the effort. Boots, ever faithful, followed Gramps to every turn, wagged his tail and barked. Alonzo gripped the railing.

"You think I haven't tried? You think I don't *want* to leave this bridge? If only I had never lost this coin. Curse that lying ragman! He cheated me, Alonzo—cheated me through and through. Sweet Lizzie said I beat him, but Lizzie's got her endings bollixed up. Ragmen don't give coins for nothing—hen nor no hen nor whatnot! I made that ragman a promise. Promised to give him back his coin when I was through or best to stay here if I didn't keep my word. How'd I know I'd lose his silly coin? Holes in the pockets day and night, a thing slips out! Not my fault his coin done disappeared."

"Ahem," said the boatman politely.

Alonzo looked to the boat, trembling against the current, and at the bridge, trembling as well. "Won't the ragman come back?" he wondered.

"Never," sighed Gramps. "They never do." His moonlit face darkened. "That dirty lying cheat! Lord, what I'd give for a good night's rest! Alonzo, I can't tell you how bone weary I've become. Every night the same: back and forth, back and forth—nowhere to rest or weary but this dang-blasted rickety bridge! It's enough to drive you *bats!*"

Alonzo could see that Gramps was just as tired as he claimed. His once broad shoulders sagged; his whiskered cheeks sank inward like withered apples. Pacing, Gramps trod the planks with the faltering steps of a marionette.

Alonzo remembered the words of the sailor, but he did not have the heart to tell Gramps that the coin had been stolen, never lost.

Instead, he glanced at the flowing stream.

"Only person who might help me is the jeweler," muttered Gramps. "The jeweler, Simon Gobbler—he's the one who etched the coin. See what he wrote there: *Liz and Gus*. The jeweler has the knack to get me off, but how'd I ever find him? I can't leave!"

Below, the boatman shifted his weight against his pole and cleared his throat rudely. His boat looked tipsy.

But then, Alonzo considered: *I know how to swim.*

"Gramps, give me the coin," said Alonzo. "I'll find the jeweler."

Gramps stopped pacing. He looked at his grandson, and his eyes went wide. "What's that you say, Alonzo? Find the jeweler? Are you daft? You'd do that for your Gramps?"

"Yes," said Alonzo. And he meant it.

Boots barked twice.

Gramps rubbed his bristly whiskers and mulled the offer long and hard. "You'd do me a powerful favor if you did. A *powerful* favor, I admit. That jeweler, Simon Gobbler, he's a rascal. No telling where you'd have to look."

Instead of arguing, Alonzo held out his hand. And Gramps, after a moment's hesitation, passed him the coin.

Gramps' eyes twinkled, and he tousled Alonzo's hair.

"Best dang grandson an old croak like me did never deserve."

"Ahem," said the boatman, "I ain't got all night."

Boots barked again to show that he was ready, and Alonzo picked him up. Carefully Alonzo climbed off the rickety bridge and took his place in the boat, toward the bow, as the boatman directed. Gramps hitched up his bibs and leaned over the railing to wish him well.

"Good luck to you, Alonzo! Thanks so much! You'll know the jeweler Gobbler by the hump of his scaly back. Tell him my name—Gus Petra—he'll remember me for sure. No dilly-dally or skylarkin'; you've only got till sunrise—don't forget! Sure wish I could come along . . . Best dang grandson an old croak like me did never deserve!"

With a wave and a whistle the boatman pulled free his pole and let the current seize the tiny craft. Alonzo waved until the boat passed a bend of willow, and then his old grandpa disappeared.

"Grandfather," mused the boatman. "Yes, I've heard of such a thing."

Alonzo showed the boatman his lucky coin and asked where he might find the fabled jeweler, but the boatman only shrugged.

"Hard to say, hard to predict. Might be here, might be there, might be a man in his underwear. I judge, if we follow the river, the old river will tell us what's best."

So Alonzo sat quiet, waiting with Boots curled at his feet as the boat floated patiently downstream.

Hour by hour slowed and passed. The boatman sang a song:

I knew a gal in '46,
Her name was Kate McCoole.
Her father was a tailor,
Her mother was a spool.
Said I to Kate, I love you dear,
Let's bind our little stitches;
Snip snap! Her daddy's scissors clacked
And clipped my salty britches!

"Land Ho," said the boatman. Done at last.

Alonzo, who had grown drowsy listening to the boatman's silly song, sat up. The boat had changed to a lily pad. The boatman was a frog. Alonzo, too, was no larger than a mouse, and Boots was the size of a cricket.

"Surprised?" asked the paddler, who now employed his feet to push them along.

They had neared a bank of the stream, a place where the reeds and cattails grew quite thickly.

"Here's where you walk," said the boatman. "Sorry I can't go with you. Them's the rules."

The lily pad bumped the muddy bank, nearly pitching Alonzo headfirst into the stream. There was no way off but to plop his sneakers into the swampy goo.

"Which way?" he questioned.

"Flip a coin," quipped the frog.

And then, croaking loudly at his own devilish jest, he dove into the stream and swam away.

Four

Nothing to do but go on, Alonzo thought.

Sure, but it wasn't easy. Alonzo and Boots fought hard to pass through the wet, bristly grass along the shore. Horsetail, thistle, and blackberry grew in abundance, forcing them to creep and crawl to avoid the sharp-horned prickers. For a time Alonzo feared they would not get anywhere at all, until at last they came upon a game trail and the way smoothed out.

Alonzo remembered the boatman's advice about flipping his coin. Heads to the left, tails to the right, or vice versa. But before he could toss, someone came.

This stranger, too, was a frog, but not like any frog Alonzo had ever seen. The frog wore a cape and floppy hat, and he carried a rag-cloth sack. With every hop the sack bounced on the frog's green shoulder, and its contents rattled.

Uncertain whether the frog was friend or foe, Alonzo hid. He might have stayed hidden until the stranger passed by, had not Boots begun to growl.

Hearing the dog, the frog threw down his bundle and crouched.

"Who's there! Come out! Thieves and brigands, attack at your peril! I am armed and well prepared!"

From his belt, the squat frog drew a dagger. He advanced threateningly toward the grass where Alonzo hid.

"Come out!" he commanded, and Alonzo thought it better to obey.

"We're lost," Alonzo explained, holding up his empty hands.

Indeed, the sight of such a tiny boy and his still tinier pooch caused the frog no small amazement. He lowered his dagger and pushed back his floppy hat. He strapped on a pair of spectacles.

"Lost? Why yes, I'd say you are. You are the tiniest boy and dog I've ever met! Come close; let me look at you. Don't be afraid. Where are you going? What's your name?"

"My name is Alonzo and this is my dog Boots. Gramps sent us to find the jeweler Simon Gobbler. Do you know him? Is he near?"

Instead of answering, the frog hunched down and croaked. "Shh! Not so loud. Don't say that name! No telling who might hear you. The jeweler Gobbler! Of course I know him! Who don't? The King hates the jeweler Gobbler. He wants to cut off his head!"

Alarmed by this news, Alonzo glanced nervously left to right. He feared there might be danger.

"Shh, no time for posturing," warned the frog, adjusting his specs. "If the King hears you mention the jeweler's name, he'll throw you into prison, or worse. Come on now, hop along."

So Alonzo, with Boots at his heels, joined the frog, whose name was Sylvester, and the three continued down the weedy trail.

Sylvester introduced himself as a minstrel who had just departed the King's court. He was a singer famed for his ballads—and my, but wasn't he mortified when Alonzo said he had never heard those tunes!

"Tell me about the jeweler," Alonzo repeated.

"Hush," said Sylvester. "Not so loud! The King hates the jeweler. Why? The King's a fool. He spent all his money for a basket of the jeweler's famous eggs. Now he's mad. What's he got reason to be mad about? It's his own stupid fault he bought those eggs! The King's greedy. He tried to cheat the jeweler, but the jeweler's just too clever for his tricks. Simon Gobbler got the bargain; now the King demands revenge."

"That's not fair," said Alonzo. "It's the king's own fault if he spent all his money on silly eggs."

Sylvester widened his eyes. "Fair? Who's to judge what's fair for folk like kings? Now you or I, if *we* had spent our money . . . Well, that's a different story—wouldn't you say? Would *you* complain?"

Alonzo thought hard before replying. He knew he just certainly might. Once he had spent four dollars on a box of baseball cards at a church rummage sale and had found not a single collectable item in the lot. That was *dumb*. Afterwards he was sorry, and he'd complained until Grandma got all red and out of sorts. That's why, when he thought about the King, he didn't quite know what to say. Maybe if *he* were a king he'd have bought some silly eggs or something worse.

While Alonzo pondered this problem, the three travelers came to a fork in the path. On one side the way became quite narrow, sloping downhill toward a mud pond where cows wallowed on hot August afternoons. The other side, broader, was a footpath well trod down. That side was easier going but more exposed.

"Which way?" asked Alonzo.

"Depends on you," said the frog. "You say you want the jeweler? My advice: ask Goody Nightsweet. Goody Nightsweet knows the way. Now that the King has spent himself poor, she's the jeweler's best customer. Can't resist his famous eggs. Trouble is: she's full of tricks."

"Where is Goody Nightsweet? Will you take me?"

"Take you? To Goody Nightsweet's? Are you nuts? Never in a hundred million years! No one goes to Goody Nightsweet unless he has to—unless he's just too tired to care."

Alonzo heard fear in Sylvester's otherwise jaunty voice.

"Take you?" said Sylvester, rolling his eyes. "Uh-uh, no way, never! But I'll show you where to go. Goody Nightsweet's house is there: down this path to the rushes. Turn left at the muddy ditch. Goody Nightsweet lives in the ferns."

The frog, Sylvester, was about to say more, when suddenly seven shadowy figures leaped from the grass.

Frogs they were—just like Sylvester. Only, unlike Sylvester, they all held arrows and bows!

Five

"Stand and deliver!" swore the attackers.

Sylvester immediately threw himself to the ground. "Mercy!" he pleaded. "Don't shoot!"

Alonzo seized Boots, who showed signs of biting. That little mutt was a puncher in a pinch. He once had nipped the sneakers of a bully.

"Stand and deliver!" swore the bandits. "Your money or your lives!"

"What money?" cried Sylvester. "We're poor as crickets, and we haven't a single copper to our names!"

This was not quite true, Alonzo thought: he did have a single copper, though he had no wish to surrender Gramps' lucky coin to a gaggle of rag-tag thieves.

He was about to tell Boots to "sic em!" when six of the seven frog banditos put down their bows.

"Aw, Robin, they're poor as us. What are we wasting our time attacking them for?"

"Cowards," said their leader, grimacing in a way that frogs do well. He sheathed his sword. "Get up," he ordered Sylvester, who had quite overdone his show of fear. "Get up," the frog repeated. "Robin Frosh is the friend of the poor. You've nothing to fear from us, unless you're rich."

"Robin Frosh! The famous outlaw!" Sylvester exclaimed.

Sylvester's surprise made the swashbuckling highwayman grin. He swelled his chest to twice its normal girth. "You see, lads, I told you—we're famous!"

"Famous! Famous indeed!" cried Sylvester. "I am Sylvester the minstrel—you've certainly heard my name? Just this evening I departed the King's court where I sang about your merry escapades. You're famous all right—a famous *thief!* The King has a reward on your head—not that he could ever pay it." As he spoke he winked at Alonzo, who understood why the King could never pay.

This news delighted the outlaw all the more, and his henchmen croaked their approval.

"Rob from the rich, give to the poor, that's our motto," said Robin Frosh.

Alonzo thought that the rascally frog had confused himself with someone else, someone more famous, but he did not think it wise to point this out. After all, Robin Frosh was dressed the part—peaked cap, Lincoln greens, longbow, quiver, etc.

"A minstrel, lads!" said Robin Frosh. "A minstrel's just what we need for our merry band. Come join us, minstrel Sylvester! All the loot and goodies you can steal; the best companions any frog could wish—no taxes, no bosses, no cares!"

"Sounds good," said Sylvester, who, like many musicians, was just a freeloader at heart.

But Alonzo wanted no part of such a deal. He reminded Sylvester of his promise.

"Show me the way to Goody Nightsweet's. I have to find the jeweler, Simon Gobbler!"

"Jeweler?" said Robin Frosh. "Did I hear you say *jeweler*? Why, the jeweler Simon Gobbler is the King's Public Enemy Number One. Higher than me— I'm Public Enemy Number Two. Are you the jeweler's friend? Do you know him? Zounds, what I would give to have that rascal Simon Gobbler in my band!"

Briefly, Alonzo explained how he needed to find the jeweler so that Gramps could get off the rickety bridge. When he mentioned the ragman, Robin frowned.

"Notorious cheats, those ragmen," Robin said. "Doesn't surprise me a bit that Gramps got stuck. As for Goody Nightsweet, your directions are wrong. She's not down there; she's elsewhere. But come with me, I'll help you find her. Old Goody and I are like this." And he held up two frog fingers, crossed.

"Hmpf," said Sylvester, who plainly thought this offer was a boast. He readjusted his spectacles.

Robin Frosh put out his hand. "Let me see the lucky coin," he said to Alonzo. "Is it gold?"

"Copper," said Alonzo. And he reluctantly let the outlaw touch the charm.

At once Robin popped the coin inside his mouth.

"Hey," cried Alonzo, "give it back!"

"Mmm, mmm," said Robin, and he spat the thing to the ground. "Don't be alarmed. Just tasting, just a test. Infallible taste buds—they can always tell a fake at just one lick. Not that one, though. It's genuine. Yep, you bet."

"Please," said Alonzo, "can't you help me?"

But at that moment one of the frogs in Robin's merry band hopped over with exciting news. A fat merchant toad was crossing the meadow on his way to the King's court.

Robin Frosh made a merry leap. "To arms, lads!" he shouted. "There's booty aplenty soon to come!"

"Wait," said Alonzo, "show me the way to Goody Nightsweet's!"

But Robin had no more time for idle chat. He strung his bow, tucked in his sword, and hopped away with his croaking, merry band. Alonzo had no choice but to come along.

The frogs laid their ambush at a place where the meadow grass grew thick. Here they waited, croaking in whispers, as the merchant toad approached with his caravan of mice.

"Let me do the talking," Robin warned.

As the merchant came near, the clever outlaw stepped into the roadway and raised his hand.

"Good evening, friend. Where ye bound?"

"Out of the way, numbskull!" scowled the merchant, who rode with three great bull frogs as his guards.

The merchant toad was fat and warty and dressed in the finest silks that wealth could buy. He rode a gray-whiskered rat, one not so fat as he, and the poor beast groaned beneath its burden.

"Your pardon," said Robin, still blocking the merchant's path. "I am but a poor man with twelve hungry children home to feed. Spare me a coin to buy some bread."

"Lazy oaf!" spat the toad. "Sell yourself to a farmer, if you're so poor! Sell your children! Sell your wife! My money's mine; I made it, and I haven't a penny for idle riff raff such as you. Out of my way, lame brain! I'm bound for the court of the King!"

And at these words the fat merchant toad shook his fist. He ordered his three body guards to remove the offensive beggar.

Robin grinned. "Pardon me, your Excellency. I had no idea you were friendly with the King. In that case, let me help you. You'll travel faster if you have a lighter load!"

So said, Robin croaked, and at once his merry band leaped from their hiding places, pounced on the merchant's body guards and disarmed them before they could resist.

"Thief! Brigand!" cried the merchant, swelling with anger and turning a hideous shade of purplish green. "You won't get away with this!"

"Won't I?" said Robin. "Well, well, we'll see about that. Look here, lads. See what our good merchant has in tow. Rob from the rich; give to the poor. That's our motto!"

Hearing these words, the fat merchant toad lost much of his fury.

"Robin Frosh!" he stammered, suddenly panicked.

Robin bowed, flourishing his cape. "Delighted and at your service! My friend, I give you a choice: surrender your wealth voluntarily, or lose it by force."

"Thief! Robber! Socialist!" croaked the toad, and his dark eyes swelled.

Suddenly a lookout raised an alarm. "Run, Robin, run! It's a trap!"

Barely had these words been shouted, when from three sides of the meadow the King's army burst through the grass. Robin's band gave a startled cry, threw down their bows, and scrammed.

"Hey!" yelled Alonzo. "Wait for me!"

The King's army attacked in force. They came on fast, hopping and shouting.

"Good luck!" Robin yelled to Alonzo as he dove into the grass. "Follow your feet—your feet will guide you! They'll get you to Goody Nightsweet's sure enough!"

"After him! Quick! He's Robin Frosh!" the soldiers cried.

Alonzo stood rooted. Suddenly, a soldier aimed an arrow at his head.

"Yikes!" cried Alonzo, and he ducked.

As frogs, the soldiers knew the meadow well, and they hopped with mighty bounds. Alonzo's short legs were no match for their martial ability.

"Hurry!" cried the soldiers. "The King will pay a fine reward for this one!"

It was indeed a race for his life, and Alonzo was losing fast. Then, as the frogs drew even, the boy crashed through a thicket of ferns and saw an enormous house.

Using the last of his strength, Alonzo ran up the walkway and banged upon the door. Boots stood at his heels, barking loudly, though his barks did little good.

"Grab him!" cried the soldiers. "He's Robin's friend!"

Three burly frogs, well scarred from waterfront brawls, thrust their webby hands at Alonzo's head. All at once the door to the house sprang open.

"Silence! What's all this ruckus! Shoo! Shoo, you rascals! Let decent people sleep!"

With a whoosh and a whisk, a broom swept down like a tornado. It caught the frogs and sent them spinning.

Alonzo cringed, afraid that he was next to fly. But the old woman wielding the broom set aside her deadly weapon. She stooped down and plucked him up.

"Hey there, you're a shortie! I've not seen one so tiny in all my years. Grow up so I can see you. That's better—*grow!* Goody Nightsweet's my name, and you are welcome. A stranger's always welcome at Goody Nightsweet's Eider Hall!"

Six

Goody Nightsweet lived in the ferns, close to a path made slippery by slugs. Her cottage was built of slime, chicken feathers, snail shells, river mud, and birch. Smoke from Goody Nightsweet's chimney curled upward to the stars. Woven through it, like frantic shadows, were bats that swooped to catch fat, glistening bugs.

Too amazed to speak, Alonzo stood and stared as he and Boots grew tall.

"There now," said Goody Nightsweet, "that's better, now you're proper. Why do you want to hop around with frogs? Those frogs are *thugs!*"

And she shook her stubby finger at the bushes, saying *thugs* so loudly that all the frogs could hear.

Clad in her starry gown and midnight apron, Goody Nightsweet stood bright as a scrubbed potato and plump as a loaf of bread. She braced her knobby hands upon her hips, smiled, and winked one eye beneath her thistly brows. Her thick hair was bound with shadow, and a scent of fresh-picked rosemary swelled her wake.

"Come in, come in, you're just in time! Always in time, always for supper. And afterwards *to bed!*"

"But I'm not sleepy," said Alonzo.

Goody Nightsweet wagged a stubby finger in his face. "Softest bed you'll ever have. Feathers plucked by my own hands. Come in. There's a bed just your size and a cushion for the mutt. Lucky that you found me when you did."

Alonzo had thought that Goody Nightsweet's cottage was cozy, but he soon saw that his eyes had played him tricks.

The room he entered was huge, palatial, vast. Unroofed, it was lit by starlight, and the stars gleamed so closely that it almost seemed possible to fetch one down with your hand. Trees, blossoming apples, were set in orderly rows down the center of Goody Nightsweet's enormous hall. Roses of every hue flowered in fragrant blossoms about their trunks.

"Why do they open at night?" Alonzo mused.

"For my guests," said Goody Nightsweet, winking. "I do my best to make it a proper home."

As she spoke, she gestured with her left hand to the curving walls on either side. All along the walls, filling every niche, were beds. Short beds, long beds, high beds, low beds, bunk beds, trundle beds, flowerbeds, single beds, double beds, queen-sized, and king. Every bed had at least one sleeper pillowed and blanketed, and some as many as ten.

Like a proud gardener, Goody Nightsweet took Alonzo's hand and led him to her beds. They stopped at one where an old man, whose gray beard was so long it flowed down over the footboard, snored loudly as a passing train.

"See here," said Goody Nightsweet, "this one's been sleeping since before I came to tend the hall. What a prodigy—he never stirs!"

She reached in her midnight apron and drew out a handful of dust. With careful swoops, Goody Nightsweet sprinkled dust over the aged sleeper, then smoothed his flowing beard and tucked his sheets. All the while she cooed like a happy dove.

"Come see," said Goody Nightsweet, "there are thousands in my hall. Busy day and night is Goody Nightsweet—never a moment's rest!"

On she led him, down endless rows of beds. At each row Goody Nightsweet fussed and fluttered, adjusting a comforter here, replacing a pillow there, and powdering one whose sleep had restless dreams.

In one bed they found a baby.

"Shh," said Goody Nightsweet, "step softly, don't be rude. This one's nearly ready to wake up. Some wake up, some keep on sleeping. Who knows why they do or don't? Some, like that old man, sleep so long and soundly they turn into roses or trees. I've had a few who changed to rocks. But this one, ah, that's the way of it—this precious little darling is nearly ready for rise and shine. See, he looks so cuddly!"

Goody Nightsweet hummed a lullaby above the sleeping infant and chucked its ruddy cheek.

"Where will he go when he wakes up?" Alonzo asked.

"Ask me no questions, I'll tell you no lies," winked Goody Nightsweet. "And see, here is the bed I made for *you!*"

An eager bed, its coverlet turned down and its pillows plumped, scampered smartly across the hall to Goody Nightsweet.

"Climb in, Alonzo, and none of your saucy backtalk."

"Woof, woof," said Boots, chasing the frisky bed behind Goody Nightsweet's ample hips.

Alonzo gripped the mutt's collar and remembered why he had come. Quickly, he took the ragman's lucky coin from his pocket, and he laid it in Goody Nightsweet's satin hand.

"*Gramps!*" said Goody Nightsweet, scrunching her eyes. "Is Gramps still on the rickety bridge?"

"He told me to find the jeweler Gobbler," Alonzo told her.

Goody Nightsweet bit the coin. "*Gramps,*" she scowled. "Good gracious, Alonzo, how can this be? Why, this is the coin that once belonged to Gramps. The jeweler Gobbler etched it—see, right there's his mark."

The bed behind Goody Nightsweet peeped out, teasing Boots, who growled.

"Shush!" said Goody Nightsweet. "You'll wake them all! Bed, go back! We'll stuff you yet. Dog, shut your yawp!"

Goody Nightsweet seized a hazel switch and shooed the pesky bed back to its corner, where its mattress sagged in disappointment. She placed the lucky coin in Alonzo's hand.

"All right, Alonzo," she nodded, "this coin does change things a bit. Never sleep on unfinished business, that's my advice. Gramps on the rickety bridge—we can't have that!"

Goody Nightsweet bustled down her rows of beds, passing by her apple trees and roses until she came to a doorway in the wall. The door was locked, but Goody Nightsweet had a key. She jangled through her pockets until she found it.

"Where we going?" asked Alonzo, afraid that Goody Nightsweet might summon another bed.

"To see my eggs. Eggs, that's what I chiefly purchase. The jeweler Gobbler makes them, and there are none finer to be had. The answer to your problem's in an egg, I'll wager that. Ah, here's the key!"

The key she wanted was a wishbone. She broke it and stuck the larger section in the lock.

Behind the door was a room, vast as the one before. And, like the other, unroofed. Strange, how warm this room did feel, Alonzo noticed—so warm that Goody Nightsweet shed her twilight shawl. The room was warm as a greenhouse in summer, filled with blossoms, and lit, at that late hour, by the moon. Moist and damp and still, the air felt so suffocating that Alonzo could hardly draw a breath.

"Where are the eggs?" he asked her.

"Silly boy. We have to hunt them."

Goody Nightsweet bustled down a path lined with crocuses, freesias, and tulips to a bed of high grown daffodils. She rooted among the stalks.

"Here's one! Not the one we want, but take a look."

She gave to Alonzo a porcelain egg whose surface was set with all manner of precious gems. The egg was warm.

"See there, on the underside, that's the jeweler's mark. He puts it on every egg he makes."

Alonzo studied the curious sigil.

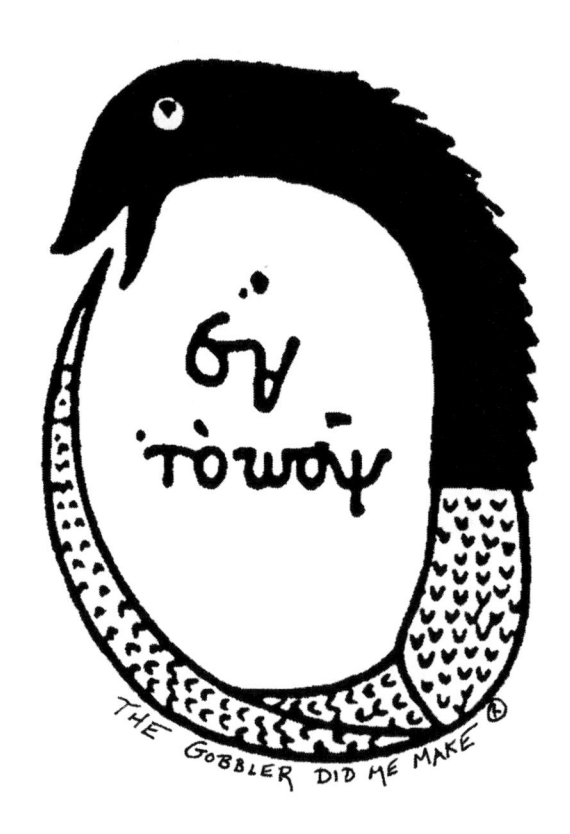

"There's another!" Goody Nightsweet exclaimed.

She gave him a second egg, this one large enough to have been laid by an ostrich. It, too, was made of porcelain and had a tiny porthole at one end.

"Peep inside," said Goody Nightsweet.

Alonzo did. To his amazement, inside the egg was another egg, and inside that one, another still. The eggs went on and on, each inside the other, each with a little window, end to end.

"Horse feathers," said Goody Nightsweet, "this egg's cracked. Try another—this one."

She handed Alonzo another egg, also of sheerest porcelain. Its shell was set with pearls.

Inside the egg Alonzo saw a workshop. A bald old man with a crooked, humpy back sat rapt beside a workbench strewn with tools. He wore a leather apron. As soon as Alonzo spied him, he stuck out his tongue.

"That's him! That's Simon Gobbler!" Alonzo exclaimed.

"Humph," said Goody Nightsweet. "Wouldn't you know it?"

Goody Nightsweet gave herself a shake, loosened her girdle, and squatted down. She placed the egg beside an iris and peered inside.

"Imagine, a woman my age crawling in the garden like a child. Let's hope my hands don't root. Hello, there! Simon Gobbler! Curse him, there he goes!"

Alonzo put his eye to the egg just in time to see the hunchback gather his tools and hurry out.

Crash! Goody Nightsweet brought a rock down on the egg, shattering it to smithereens.

"Too late, he got away!" the woman cried.

Goody Nightsweet struggled to her feet. Her face was red, her eyes hot as carbuncles. She shook from head to foot.

"It's up to you, Alonzo—the Gobbler's gone. He's the slyest, craftiest jeweler that ever lived. The pest! If it weren't for his eggs, I'd have put him to bed long ago—and well he knows it! I've a good mind to break every egg in this garden—that would teach him a lesson he would not soon forget!"

At that moment Boots began to bark. Amidst a bed of high-grown lilies the dog had found the most enormous egg Alonzo had ever seen. The egg, porcelain like the rest, was set with jewels and hammered gold.

The egg was taller than Alonzo, and instead of a window it had a door. The door was marked with the same curious sigil that Alonzo had seen on other eggs.

"There," said Goody Nightsweet, "leave it to man's best friend. He's found the door to Simon Gobbler's workshop. That smaller egg was just a trick. Go in, Alonzo, the door is never locked. Show the jeweler your coin and tell him I'm waiting for Gramps. But be careful, the jeweler's prices are high. He'll not do you favors for nothing, I promise that!"

She pushed on the door, and it squeaked open.

"Quick!" she commanded, and she flicked her hazel switch.

Seven

The door to the egg opened and shut so quickly that Boots nearly pinched his curly tail. And when it closed, it was gone.

Alonzo found himself not in the jeweler's workshop, as he had expected, but on a road, a dirt road much like the one that eased by Grandma's farm. On either side of the road were fields of wheat full grown and ready for the harvest. The sun stood high at noontime, though a cricket chirped the hour at three o'clock.

How time does fly, thought Alonzo, remembering Gramps on the rickety bridge.

The road was low and the wheat had grown so high that Alonzo relied on Boots to choose the way. The dog sniffed and wagged his tail, scampered a few steps one way, then doubled back. A light breeze rustled the wheat and brought to Alonzo's ears a snatch of song.

> *The merry widow Underhill*
> *Keeps spiders in her clocks,*
> *Stitches cornhusks for a dress*
> *Cuts holes in strangers' socks.*
> *A moldy pumpkin is her home,*
> *Daughter Jill must sweep it;*
> *Jack the husband drowned at sea*
> *A better man will never be*
> *Unless the widow twists the key*
> *To Simon Gobbler's lock.*

Not far down the road, the wheat parted at a hillside. There, beneath a lone and shady oak tree, Alonzo saw a gang of harvesters taking their noontime rest. Twelve of the harvesters were asleep, but two—an old man and a boy—sat with their backs to the tree and shared a jug. It was the old man who sang. When he saw Alonzo, he put down his jug and waved.

"Hello, stranger! Where ye bound? Come rest with us this noontime. It's a cruel sun that will bake your hatless head. Come, eat and drink!"

Alonzo noticed that the old man looked much like the ancient sleeper he had seen but a moment ago in Goody Nightsweet's Eider Hall. Like the sleeper, this old harvester's beard was of prodigious length. Unbound, it fell a goodly yard beyond his feet.

Hungry and thirsty, Alonzo started up the hill, passing over the bodies of the twelve exhausted harvesters. Flies buzzed noisily about their sweat-stained shirts, making a fine counterpoint to the concert of snores, snuffles, and wheezing grunts.

"Greetings!" said the old man. "Come sit for a while beneath our shady tree. My sons are asleep—except for this one, and he's an idiot who never shuts his god-cursed eye."

The boy he referred to had indeed but one good eye, and this one quite awkwardly right in the middle of his forehead.

The boy was glad for his father's attention. He blinked his one eye proudly and laughed, although neither Alonzo nor the father had made a joke.

Annoyed, the old man chased the boy from the shade with a swift kick of his bootless foot. The boy ran to the edge of the wheat, and there he squatted, braying like a mule, and daring his father to pelt him with acorns fallen from the tree, which his father gladly did from time to time.

"Ah," said the old man, stretching amply, "it's a life if you can stand it."

He took up his scythe and ran one callused finger along the blade, prompting Alonzo to ask the question uppermost in his mind.

"How do you harvest with a beard as long as that?"

The old man laughed—a hearty, toothless guffaw—and he showed Alonzo how he wound up his beard like a turban about his head when he went to swing his scythe.

"Better than a hat," he assured him.

Then the old man offered Alonzo and Boots some of his unleavened rye and gave them limewater to drink. Refreshed, Alonzo thought it best to get on with his search.

"Excuse me; do you know the jeweler Gobbler?"

But the mere mention of the jeweler's name woke the old man's twelve sons from their sound slumber. Those who wore hats sneezed and snapped their brims, while their long-bearded father bowed and scraped the ground in frank oblation.

"Simon Gobbler's our master! He owns the wheat!"

The twelve sons, perceiving that a stranger was in their midst, gathered around the tree and stared with wide eyes and gaping mouths at Alonzo. They were all of differing age and size: one a teenager, another nearly as old as the old man. They wore hemp shirts bound to their waists with hanks of yellow rope, and their coarse hair and beards were matted and flecked with stubble.

"Follow your feet!" said one. "Your feet will guide you. Simon Gobbler's the friend of feet."

Immediately the old man and his twelve sons began to argue whether it was better for Alonzo to find his way with his shoes on or off. Alonzo noted that the older brothers were barefoot, while the younger all wore boots.

"Considering his age, he should keep them on," said a middle-aged harvester. "Besides, his shoes have so many holes that his toes will have no trouble peeping out."

This question settled, the men took their scythes and began to whet the blades.

"Thank you for your help," said Alonzo politely.

"Not so fast," replied the old man. "You have eaten our bread and swallowed our water; you cannot leave until you work."

"Aye," said the others, "a year and a day hard labor!"

Suddenly, a circle of bearded men surrounded Alonzo.

"Let me go!" he exclaimed. "I can't work for you! Gramps is stuck on the rickety bridge!"

But the twelve harvesters and their father only laughed. "He chased Dumbkin into the wheat! Let him take the idiot's place! One good turn deserves another! Right-o, lads!"

"Please, please!" cried Alonzo, "let me go! I have to find the jeweler Gobbler!"

Once more, the mention of the jeweler's name set the harvesters busy with bows, respectful scrapings, sneezes, and snorts.

"Hmm," said one, "we dare not anger the Master . . ."

"He owns the wheat!"

"Let him *buy* his way out of it!"

"That's right! If he won't work, let him *pay!*"

But Alonzo had no money except for his precious coin.

He began to cry.

"There, there," said the old man, wiping Alonzo's tears with his lengthy beard, "everyone's got something. Fair is fair, and one good turn deserves another. You'll have to trade. Maybe you can teach us *a game.*"

"That's right," said the twelve harvesters, "if he won't pay, let him teach!"

Alonzo thought hard. The only games he knew required proper equipment, and here was nothing useful but a wheat field and a tree.

"I've got it, I'll teach you to bat!"

"Delightful idea!" exclaimed the harvesters, and they threw aside their scythes.

Alonzo picked up a fallen oak limb, trimmed it down, and found a suitable stone. Choosing one of the harvesters at random, he made him pitch. Indeed, once the fellow got the hang of it he did quite well.

Crack! Alonzo connected with a fine line drive. The stone went flying into the wheat, where Dumbkin chased it.

All was extremely quiet. Then, like an explosion, the harvesters erupted into cheers.

"I'm next!"

"No, me!"

"Oldest first!"

"I was in line before you were!"

"Quiet!" roared the old man.

Soon the harvesters were lined up in order of height and were busy pelting stones at one-eyed Dumbkin. In a few minutes they had batted away every stone upon the hill.

"More, more, we want more!"

But, search though they might, there were no more stones to be had.

"I've got it," said one of the cleverest. "We'll use our *heads!*"

And quick as a flash he seized his scythe and lopped off the head of his brother.

Swish, swash, swish! Each of the twelve soon lost his head. But did that stop them? No. Headless, they batted all the better.

The father laughed, for the game was splendid. Standing as pitcher, he tossed each son his head. Crack! Zing! The heads flew out like missiles. Each swing a pure home run!

"My thanks to you, stranger," said the old harvester, "you've taught us a wonderful game. We've not had such fun in ages! You may leave."

The old man shook hands with Alonzo and set him on his way, while the twelve headless harvesters waved their scythes in fond farewell.

"Follow your toes! Your toes will guide you! Simon Gobbler's the friend of feet!"

But, despite this good advice, all too soon Alonzo's toes fell into discord. At an unmarked crossroads he had to wait while the right foot abused the left. A cloud covered the sun, and the afternoon felt like thunder.

All at once Boots began to bark. He bared his teeth in a snarl that made Alonzo forget his squabbling toes. With a shiver, the boy looked up.

Shuffling down the road, swathed in a tempest, came a ragman.

The ragman had no face, no hands, no hair, nor any feet. Toeless, he could not find his way. Like a tattered scarecrow, the ragman lurched blindly toward Alonzo, whose ten good toes, shamed by the spectacle, had ceased their confusion and were silent. The ragman had no mouth, no ears, no eyes, no nose, nor anything to understand with. Four crows, cawing, mocked him on the wing.

East! said one.
West! said his brother.
How many? said a third.
Three pennies! said another.

But Alonzo had only one penny, and he dared not spend it. Indeed, he felt too terrified to budge.

Closer and closer came the ragman. He stretched out his ragged arms—*the hands were tatters!* Torn and stained, they flapped like faded banners from his wrists.

Boots growled his fiercest snarl. As the ragman neared, the feisty mutt lunged for the ragman's leg. Before Alonzo could blink, the dog tore away a patch of tattered burlap.

Rrripp!

The ragman staggered. The crows flew up.

"Murder, murder!" they cawed, alarming the headless harvesters, who ran down the hill with gleaming scythes.

"Boots, stop it! Stop!"

The dog would not. Growling, he attacked again, tearing free another patch of rag.

The ragman raised his arms. He lurched to the right and to the left like a drunk at sea. The grey rags of his chest flapped open. A chicken leaped out. It ran off squawking. A rooster followed after.

All at once Alonzo's toes made up their minds. As the ragman staggered, Alonzo's feet leaped forward, running their fastest straight into the field of ripened wheat.

The harvesters shouted—"Stop! It's forbidden!"—but Alonzo's toes would not. The wheat, full grown and golden, swelled up in endless waves. On he rushed, crushing the slender stalks, not minding how they fell. The wheat grew larger, impossibly tall. It rose above his head, a flood of grain!

Breathless, he continued until the wheat blocked out the sky. He swam hard against the grain, which grew so thick he lost his breath. How long could his toes continue?

Boots was the one who made them stop. The dog, ever close to Alonzo's heels, collided with his legs. Alonzo staggered, stumbled, and went down hard, rolling like a barrel down down down the gentle slope of that golden hill, flattening a swath.

"Ouch!" he exclaimed, more startled than hurt.

"One hour, one hour," warned a cricket.

Eight

He must have lost his way.

Standing, Alonzo saw that he had fallen not in a wheat field but by a curb—a stone street fogged and silent, lit by gas. Far away, concealed by smoky rooftops, a clock tower ceased its hourly chime. The time was night.

Clip clop, clip clop—the steady hammering was not the beat of his heart. On the cobbled street beside him, a horse passed by. Starved and skeletal, each hoof clop sent a tremor through the shanks. The horse was hitched to a wagon, and on the wagon rode a man. A tinker, by the looks of him—his rickety cart was loud with clattering pans.

"Whoa! Whoa!" swore the tinker, pulling his reins. But before his wagon slowed, Alonzo ran.

All the city lay in slumber, and on every house the shutters were tightly latched. Alonzo followed his feet, which led him swiftly: upstairs, downstairs, under, out, and through: down alleyways, boulevards, avenues, and squares—at last to a broad plaza with a fountain. An old woman sat by this fountain, stirring the water evenly, every night. As soon as she saw him, she winked.

At the western edge of the plaza, a large set of stairs led upward through soot-stained columns where flocks of dusty pigeons crept and cooed. The stairs stopped before a door—enormous, carved of oak. A lesser door was fitted in its middle. And a smaller door in that. The least of these three doorways bore a sign, which read:

SIMON GOBBLER'S
WORLD MUSEUM OF EGGS

*

Hours: Sunset to Sunrise
And Upon Arrangement
7 Days a Week

*

Entry Price: Children, $1.00
Adults, 1 Penny
SENIORS NEVER CHARGED

*

Admission Free To the Public
Every Friday

*

Closed On
Christmas, Easter, Halloween

Alonzo set his hand to the least of these three doors. The door swung open easily, its hinges thickly greased.

The door admitted him to a vestibule. Before him stood a wooden desk with a revolving rack of postcards black and white. Each postcard pictured an egg. The desk was bare, the chair behind it empty. A sign on the wall said: SHOUT!

Alonzo did. Weakly, of course. As best he could.

At once a frog in a red train conductor's cap, shiny buttoned vest, and faded green leggings hopped from his resting place in a bucket and clambered on to the desk.

"About time you got here!" he chided.

"Robin Frosh!"

The frog bowed, honored by recognition. He tipped his hat then drew from the watch pocket of his vest a golden cricket fastened to a golden chain.

"Time, time," chirped the cricket.

"Robin, how did you get here?" asked Alonzo.

"Same as you," the frog said pertly, "I followed my feet. Do you like my new uniform? Ain't it swell? Goody Nightsweet got me the job! And a good job it is—better than lurking in the meadow, dodging the King's archers day and night. See what I do? I count the guests. Twenty-five-thousand-eight-hundred visitors—and you're the last! Go in, you're already ticketed. Goody Nightsweet bears the expense."

He pointed Alonzo toward a pair of revolving doors.

"Go in. The museum closes in an hour. Hurry, don't waste your time."

Alonzo, with Boots at his heels, pushed through the swinging doors and entered the museum's central hallway.

Here, sad to say, his toes lost all sense of direction, perhaps because the museum was so vast. There were so many people milling about that the scene reminded Alonzo of one of those well-attended pancake breakfasts at Grandma's church.

The hall, well lit by fluorescents, was festooned with flags and bunting, and all along its length vendors had set up shop. The smell of barbecued spare ribs sweetened the air, and in the distance a volunteer band played waltzes off key for dancers who didn't notice. Children ran to and fro dressed in their Sunday best. Each carried a little basket filled with chocolate rabbits, plastic grass, and eggs. A man in a bunny costume gave Alonzo a coupon; above, a trapeze artist did somersaults, risking life and limb for scarce, indifferent applause.

"Guided tours!" a straw-hat barker barked. "Tours of the museum—a penny a head!"

But Alonzo wanted no part of such an offer. Instead, he chose a quiet passage to his left, a small, boy-sized corridor whose archway bore the title:

WORLD HISTORY OF THE EGG.

It was, as the title suggested, an exhibition of eggs from earliest prehistory to present day. Each egg was displayed in an individual glass case lit by glowworms. There were stone eggs, wooden eggs, copper, bronze, and iron eggs; bamboo eggs and grass eggs, crystal eggs and horned eggs, eggs woven of cobweb that glowed with unnatural light, eggs made of rubber bands, human hair, or foil; plastic eggs, mechanical eggs, and eggs of every precious jewel or gemstone known to man—as well as eggs of every creature known to lay them, living or extinct. It was the finest natural history of egg that Alonzo had ever witnessed. Indeed, had the night been longer he would have enjoyed spending more time in this display. The candied eggs were most especially intriguing, Alonzo thought.

But Boots, with a nose for business, kept Alonzo on course by darting down a corridor that led to another exhibit, this one of eggs much like those Alonzo had seen in Goody Nightsweet's Eider Hall.

These eggs were not displayed in cases; they were arranged in various nests. The nests, of course, were made by people not by birds, and because the eggs were of all different sizes, the nests were of all different sizes, too.

Like the eggs at Goody Nightsweet's Eider Hall, these eggs were porcelain and were embellished with jewels. Each egg had a little window at the narrowest end, a porthole through which the curious might peep.

Alonzo wandered down the rows of nested eggs until he came to one which bore a pregnant inscription:

> *Sweet visitor, who doth intend*
> *To view the scene that lies within,*
> *Know, your kindness is the charm*
> *That grants you pleasure, never harm.*
> *Forbear, forbear harsh words to speak*
> *Lest by your censure, shells you break.*
> *Brittle are we, lifeless without,*
> *Love alone shall make us sprout.*

While Boots busied himself sniffing the scents from all the forgotten visitors who had trooped by that display, Alonzo placed his eye to the tiny porthole at the egg's narrowest end.

To his surprise, he saw Gramps, still alone and pacing the rickety bridge.

"Gramps!"

Gramps screwed up his eyes toward the moon.

"Alonzo?" he said, disbelieving.

"I'm here, I'm here! Gramps, can't you see me! I'm in Simon Gobbler's museum—Goody Nightsweet let me in! Look, Gramps, I've got the coin! The lucky charm!"

Gramps, however, rubbed his bald head, hitched up his overalls, and looked perplexed.

"Alonzo?"

"Gramps! Gramps! Can't you see me? You're in the egg!"

"Humph," said the old man. "This rickety bridge is driving me bats!"

And he once again began to pace.

Saddened and distressed, Alonzo was of half a mind to break the egg, as he had seen Goody Nightsweet do in her garden, but he feared two things: one, that in breaking the egg he might injure Gramps; and two, that he might offend the museum management.

"Woof, woof!" said Boots, who had chased a pesky cricket under a case.

"Heel," said Alonzo, but the dog would not. He growled and barked more fiercely.

Ignoring the noise, Alonzo again placed his eye to the egg, hoping to catch Gramps' attention.

But Gramps was gone. Instead of Gramps, Alonzo saw the front porch of Grandma's house. Only, it was not the front porch as he had known and left it, but the front porch as it had been once long ago.

The sycamore told him. This sycamore, which stood alongside Grandma's porch, was presently so large that Keith the gardener had nailed a platform to its sturdy, shaggy boughs—all for Alonzo to play in. Yet, the tree inside the egg was very young, only a sapling.

Squinting, Alonzo saw a young man walk toward the porch. He was only in his teens. Halfway to the steps the young man halted. He stood still and shifted his weight.

Alonzo felt there was something terribly familiar about that young man, and in a moment he knew why. The young man was Gramps, but Gramps as Gramps had been once long ago.

Gramps stood still, swayed from foot to foot, slicked his hair and hitched up his pants. He fished in his pocket and took out something Alonzo could not see. Whatever it was, it was very precious, for Gramps palmed it and brought it to his lips. He blew on his hand three times, whispered words Alonzo could not hear, smoothed back his cowlick, and proceeded toward the porch.

"Woof, woof!" said Boots, impatiently clawing to reach the cricket he had trapped.

Distracted, Alonzo rubbed his eyes and peered again.

Time moved quite swiftly inside the egg. In the moment it had taken Alonzo to blink, Gramps had gone to the house, knocked, and been admitted. Now he sat on the porch swing with a girl—and indeed, she was only a girl, not yet a woman, though Alonzo knew at once she was Grandma Liz.

Gramps and Grandma sat hand in hand, swinging in the porch swing and not at all very fast. Grandma had her eyes cast down, a habit she still affected from time to time. Alonzo smiled, until all at once Gramps did something very rude. Boldly, he placed his arm around Grandma's shoulder, drew her fast to him, and smooched her on the lips.

"Yech!" said Alonzo.

"Woof, woof!" said Boots.

"Time," chirped the cricket near his feet.

All changed inside the egg. The tree grew tall; the porch fell empty; the swaying swing collapsed.

"Gramps! Gramps! Where's Gramps!"

Inside the egg, another man appeared. It was the cow vet, Dr, Sugar. Dr. Sugar walked right to the window through which Alonzo peeped, and he put his eye to the glass.

"*Eggs?*" said the doctor, in his reassuring southern drawl. "Eggs? Eggs? I love 'em. Boiled, scrambled, poached, or fried!"

Alonzo blinked. Dr. Sugar blinked as well. The cricket, which had hidden under the display case, leaped free with a sudden bound. Surprised, Alonzo saw it hop into his egg.

"Stop!" yelled Alonzo, and he shook the display.

To his utter dismay and horror, the egg, through which he'd been peeping, fell to the hard museum floor. It shattered, and as it broke, the cricket reared up beside him and the walls of the exhibit suddenly changed.

Alonzo staggered back, while Boots barked and yipped. The walls of the museum stretched like taffy. They swelled and folded and sagged.

"Time, time," chirped the cricket, grown larger now, quite big.

"Why," said Alonzo, "you're not a cricket!"

"That's right," said the cricket as he shucked aside his cricket mask. "I'm not a cricket, never was a cricket, and never hope to be! Greetings, friend, and welcome to my workshop. The jeweler, Simon Gobbler, at your service!"

Nine

Frustrated at losing his cricket, Boots barked furiously at the hunchback's spindly legs.

"My, my," said the jeweler, "your little friend's a pest."

And before Alonzo could say please and thank you, the wily jeweler worked his art and banished poor Boots to the inside of an egg, one of the many thousands he had stored on the shelves of his endless workshop.

"Give me back my dog!" Alonzo yipped.

"Woof, woof!" answered Boots, though faintly, for the egg did quiet him quite a bit.

"Peace," said the hunchback, "your little dog is fine. See for yourself if you don't believe me."

Alonzo put his eye to the tiny porcelain egg in which Boots was kenneled. The jeweler was correct. Inside the egg Alonzo saw a red fire hydrant and an oak tree filled with squirrels. All the squirrels chattered loudly and ran up and down the tree. Boots was not barking to get out; he was barking with pleasure.

"He'll be quite content until we're done," said Simon Gobbler. "I really can't allow animals free run of my workshop—not with all these eggs. I'm sure you get my drift."

Alonzo stared at the room in which he found himself. It, too, was an egg, or at least the rounded walls and ceiling did suggest so.

"But where's the museum?" Alonzo asked.

"Oh, it's out there somewhere," said Simon Gobbler. "Things stay pretty much where they're supposed."

As he spoke, the jeweler took a clean rag from his workbench and, wetting it, began to scrub the sticky cricket makeup from his face. Alonzo stared with fascination as the long cricket feelers came away.

Though completely a man, Simon Gobbler looked strange. His large humped back reminded Alonzo of a tortoise. His legs, in their short, leather britches, were knobby-kneed and bowed, while his long spindly arms looked frail as withes. Stranger still, thought Alonzo, was the appearance of his head. Not a speck of hair did he possess. The jeweler, Simon Gobbler, was as bald as the proverbial egg.

"You see," said Simon Gobbler, "here is where I do my work. I dare say the world would beat a path to my door if I gave it any hint where to find me. Goody Nightsweet, she'd especially like to get in! Can't resist me—or my eggs! Buys more eggs than anyone I know. What a hoarder! I can just imagine all the lies she must have told you—she's so fiercely jealous of my art."

"Please," said Alonzo, remembering why he had come, "Gramps sent me. He needs your help."

"*Gramps on the rickety bridge?*" said Simon Gobbler. "Good gracious, is *Gramps* still on his feet? One moment. I'll check my lists."

So said, the jeweler Gobbler lifted to his workbench a large Easter basket filled with colored eggs. The eggs were cleverly constructed to hinge apart. Some of the eggs held baby chickens, and these ran away peeping as soon as they were freed. But some of the eggs held ledgers.

Simon Gobbler lifted out one tiny ledger with a pair of tweezers, and he read it with an enormous ivory-handled glass.

"When you're in business as long as I am, you have to keep good lists. You never know when a customer might have a complaint. All work warranted for a lifetime. Let's see . . . what year did Gramps acquire his famous egg?"

"It's not an egg," said Alonzo, "it's a coin!"

And he took the precious token from his pocket.

Simon Gobbler laughed, showing for the first time that his mouth was toothless as a new born babe's.

"Land sakes, sonny, you don't suppose I issued warranties on those! A ragman's lucky charm—now there's a corker! I got out of novelties years ago. Decades, to be exact. Never made a nickel in the trade. Eggs are my bread and butter. Those love charms earned me nothing but complaints. No, no, I can't guarantee and never did guarantee those silly coins! Sold the whole inventory to a ragman—I can't recall his name; perhaps he didn't have one. They seldom do."

"Please," said Alonzo, nearing tears, "Gramps is stuck on the rickety bridge!"

"Hmm," said Simon Gobbler, "not my beeswax. Now, if Gramps could use an egg . . ."

"Not an egg! Gramps is *stuck!*"

Simon Gobbler scrunched up his eyes and sucked his purplish lips. His bald, egg-shaped face turned very red. "Oh, oh," he muttered, "why can't they just leave me to work in peace!"

"Please, please!" begged Alonzo, "you've got to help him—you've got to set Gramps free—you simply must!"

"Ah," scowled the jeweler, "what's to say? Very well, very well, but stop your crying. I'll do what I can to help, but for a *price.*"

Alonzo wiped his eyes and drew a breath. He remembered Goody Nightsweet's warning that the jeweler Gobbler's price was very steep.

He swallowed and set his jaw.

"I'll do anything for Gramps."

"Sold!" said the jeweler. "Give me the coin!"

Fearful that he had agreed to some terrible bargain, Alonzo hesitated to hand over the token, but the jeweler moved very swiftly and snatched it from his hand.

"First we must melt it!"

In the corner of his workshop, on a pedestal, was a furnace shaped like a frog. Simon Gobbler cranked open the frog furnace mouth, squinted against the heat, and threw the lucky coin inside. The frog began to shake and bounce. Steam shot out of its nostrils.

"Stand back, we've got a live one!" the jeweler warned.

All at once the frog croaked loudly and belched the red-hot coin. The coin flew like a shooting star into a tub of water, which promptly boiled and hissed.

The jeweler fetched it out with a pair of tongs.

"There," he said, "you see, the script has vanished! The coin is completely blank. A few minutes more and we'll be done."

Carefully, the jeweler laid the coin upon his workbench then called to his assistance a pair of fiery salamanders, who, with their quick, acidic tongues, etched a curious sigil. Simon Gobbler worked until both sides of the coin were freshly etched. Then he smiled and wiped his hands upon his apron.

"Well, well," he said, "and just in time for breakfast! A better job than that you'll seldom see."

He flipped the coin to Alonzo then stooped to remove his shoes.

"Wait," said Alonzo. "How much do I owe?" As he spoke, his voice trembled, for he feared some evil price.

But the jeweler, with his toes set free, only laughed.

"What goes around comes around!" the Master said.

And before Alonzo could say bananas, the hunchback put his big toes to his lips. Turning red, he began to suck, first the toes, then the feet, then the calves. Clearly, the jeweler meant to suck himself away.

"Wait!" cried Alonzo, "don't leave yet!"

On the rounded wall of the workshop, a large cuckoo clock began to chime. A tiny door burst open, and two mechanical crickets dressed like dolls marched smartly out. One a wife, the other a husband, they sang an hourly duet.

Sun is risen, night is fled,
Shatter! All you sleepy heads!

"Mmm, mmm," said Simon Gobbler, sucking right up to his thighs, and redder, indeed, than any red tomato.

Red, too, glowed the walls of Simon Gobbler's workshop, for outside, as the crickets truly sang, the great Grand-daddy Sun had shown his face.

"Mmm-bye, mmm-bye," said the jeweler as Alonzo gaped and stared. With one prodigious pop, Simon Gobbler sucked his torso right into his mouth. And disappeared.

And with that the workshop went mad.

Abandoned by their maker, all the eggs in the workshop began to hatch at once. A swarm of chicks and crickets burst from the shells. The frog furnace leaped free of its pedestal; it hopped about, upsetting furniture right and left. Boots chased a squirrel out from his porcelain kennel, and broken shells rained down on Alonzo's head. Worse, with a sound more terrible than any earthquake, the floor to the workshop fractured end to end. Out of the many cracks and fissures, tulips reared their global heads.

"Boots! Boots! Grandma! Help!"

With a deafening *POP!* the ceiling to the workshop split apart, revealing the bluest of blue skies and a face so large it eclipsed the rising sun.

"Alonzo Petra, you scamp! So there you are! I had to crack a dozen till I found you!"

Goody Nightsweet, quite enormous and fresh from her evening rounds, reached in her stubby fingers and picked Alonzo out of the egg. She popped him in her apron pocket head first and feet wriggling.

"Really, Alonzo, you've been up far too late for a child your age! To bed, to bed, and no more saucy backtalk!"

Alonzo righted himself and peered over the edge of the apron pocket. He was back in the hall of beds, and there, tucked neatly beneath a plush feather comforter, was Gramps.

Gramps waved as Alonzo went by.

"Thanks and blessings, Alonzo! You did swell! The jeweler, Simon Gobbler, I told you he had the knack! Got me off that rickety bridge, and just in time—I'm nearly bats! I'll remember this forever—rest certain on that!"

"Gramps! Gramps! Help me! I don't want to go to bed!"

But before he could pull himself from the apron pocket, Goody Nightsweet flicked her hazel switch and summoned to her side the frisky bed whose sheets and pillows were just Alonzo's size.

"Good night, Sweet Prince," cooed Goody Nightsweet, as she plopped him on the mattress and tucked him in.

"Gramps! Gramps! Grandma! Help!"

But Gramps was snoring soundly in his bed.

Ten

"Heavens to Betsy, what a sleeper!"

Alonzo opened one groggy eye in time to see Grandma, dressed smartly in her Sunday best, hurry into his bedroom. She slam-closed the window with a bang. Outside, trees swayed wildly in the strong, equinoctial wind. The rising sun shone radiant through the glass.

"Not too windy for churchin'," Grandma said. "Get dressed, Alonzo. Food's frying. No dilly-dally. Not today!"

Boots jumped off the bed and followed Grandma down the stairs, eager to chow. Alonzo, yawning, staggered off to Grandma's bathroom then searched for something to wear. He had trouble doing his buttons, and his socks refused to match. By the time he got his clip-on necktie fastened to his white and starchy shirt, Grandma was yelling and banging a dented pot.

Alonzo hurried down the stairs, shoelaces flapping, stumbled on the landing, and banged the wall.

Halfway to the kitchen he heard a honk in the yard. Dr. Sugar, driving his blue Impala with the CB antenna on the back, had arrived as he had promised, right on time.

Grandma's food was fit to fly as Dr. Sugar slammed the screen door and sauntered in. Smiling, the good doctor went to the sink and washed his hands.

"Morning, Liz! Morning, Alonzo! Mmm, mmm, smell that breakfast! Eggs, how I love 'em! Boiled, scrambled, poached, or fried!"

He was, as Grandma had told him often, the sweetest mannered gentleman in the county.

Alonzo's appetite was huge. Under Grandma's approving gaze, he ate two helpings of everything—eggs, pancakes, bacon, grits, and toast—and he washed the whole thing down with floods of orange juice.

"Bless me," said Dr. Sugar, "I do believe that youngster grew an inch! Alonzo, hop over here aside my chair. There's something fair peculiar in my pocket."

Dr. Sugar reached in the hip pocket of his Harris tweedy coat and took out a half dozen wax packs of baseball cards, just the kind Alonzo loved to collect.

"Well, will you look at that!" said Dr. Sugar. "Who'd have ever thought those cards were in there?"

Alonzo took the packs, eager to see which players were inside. Grandma leaned closer. She, too, loved to collect.

And indeed, the cards were rare.

"Sweetest mannered gentleman in the county," Grandma said.

Dr. Sugar eased back from the table, smiled at the flattery, and mouse-like smoothed the hairs of his moustache.

"Thanks, Liz," said Dr. Sugar. "And if I may say so, you're mighty sweet yourself."

Alonzo sopped up a puddle of gooey syrup and fingered his brand new cards, while Grandma lowered her fine Kentucky eyes. An old windup ticker struck its chimes.

"*Time, time,*" chirped a cricket, well hidden beneath the fridge.

On the way to Grandma's church they passed the river, brown with all the muck from recent rain. Alonzo pressed his face right up to the backseat window, squinting as they neared the rickety bridge.

No one stood at the railing. No boatman dared to ply that stream today.

Dr. Sugar worked a game on the front dash radio, while Grandma let the breezes tease her hair.

"Why you smiling?" Grandma asked him.

Alonzo didn't say. He watched as they passed the empty bridge.

Far behind Alonzo at the farmhouse, Boots lay curled in sunlight, dreaming of squirrels that scampered up and down with endless chatter on trees that grew gigantic inside eggs. Outside those porcelain shells in halls of roses, Gramps reposed like Boots in sheer contentment, plump as a new-born infant—asleep in Goody Nightsweet's eider bed.

THE TALE OF THE SHINING PRINCESS

In a cabin by the shores of the western sea, a fisherman lived with his wife. Each morning if the sea was calm, the fisherman rowed out upon the waves and spread his nets. For years he had fished, and the ocean had sustained him. Though poor, he had never starved, and he felt blessed.

Yet, as the years passed and the fisherman grew older, more and more often there were days when his nets came up slack.

At night by the cabin fire, he confessed his fears to his wife.

"Ah, my dearest, what shall we do? Soon I will be too old to do my work. Each year the catch seems deeper. Each year I feel smaller, but the ocean is ever vast. If only we had a son—a son who could help me, a son who could mend and haul my nets."

His words made the woman very sad. They had tried many times to have children; two had died in childbirth, and one had drowned.

"It is too late," she sighed. "We are too old. Heaven must provide if you cannot."

"Wife," scoffed the fisherman, "those words are easily said. What will they mean when we are hungry? What will they mean when I can no longer fish? Will heaven provide for us then?"

That night the fisherman's wife could not sleep. She worried and tossed.

As the old fisherman lay snoring, the fisherman's wife rose from their bed of marriage and crept to the window of their cottage to a place where the full moon shone brightly from above. There she had placed a rickety loom. As her husband slept, she sat at her loom and wove. She spoke to herself softly as she worked.

"What shall become of us when my husband is too old? The poor are despised; the defenseless suffer; the rich care only for themselves . . ."

Her thoughts had no end. The moon shone in upon her. It played upon her loom.

Come see . . . the moon seemed to whisper.

Past midnight, the old woman stopped weaving and left the cabin. She wrapped a blue shawl about her shoulders to keep herself warm.

She walked to the sea. The sand gleamed silver in the starlight; the shoreline rocks were damp and midnight black. The air smelled thickly of seaweed and salt spray, and to the west the moon shone low on the horizon—so low, it looked as though it floated like an ark. The ocean rolled before her, rustling the sand.

As the old woman stood there pondering, a wave broke just in front of her. She had seen it rolling toward her from the west. The wave washed a curious object to her feet.

Startled, the woman bent down.

On the sand, amid the debris of broken shells and seaweed, the woman saw a light. The light—as bright as the light from a candle—shone from a blue-white pearl. The pearl was round and smooth, the size of a marble. It gleamed like ice. "Ah," thought the woman, "what good fortune!"

Clutching the beautiful pearl in her woolen shawl, she hurried home. Her husband slept so soundly that she did not dare to wake him up. Instead, she hid the pearl, still wrapped in her woolen shawl, under a basket beside her loom. And then she lay down. She felt tired, so very tired, and her body relaxed.

That night, her dreams were very peaceful.

Her husband slept soundly, too. Well past the hour that he long had been accustomed to gather his nets, he finally stirred. At once he blinked with surprise.

"Wife," he exclaimed, shaking the old woman's shoulder. "Wake up! Look! What has happened? Who is that stranger in our home?"

The old woman rubbed her eyes.

She and her husband were no longer alone.

In the corner of the cabin near a window facing south, beside the old woman's rickety loom, a maiden slept. The maiden lay on a bed of dried seaweed that the woman had placed there the day before. She lay curled beneath the old woman's tattered shawl.

"Who's that?" said the fisherman. "Where did she come from?"

The strange maiden did not stir. She appeared to be only fifteen or sixteen years of age. Her beauty was perfect—so perfect that it made the old fisherman shiver. The maiden's hair was long and glistening black. Her skin was smooth and unblemished. Even a goddess would have envied her. And yet, she slept quite humbly on the earthen floor with her head pillowed on her forearm and her face completely peaceful and relaxed—naked, save for the old woman's tattered shawl.

Struck dumb, the fisherman and his wife gaped at their visitor, until suddenly the old woman remembered the shimmering pearl that the ocean waves had brought to her feet the night before. In trembling words she recounted her adventure. But when she was done, the fisherman scowled. He did not see the point of it, and he wished that his wife had taken better care of the precious catch.

"She must be a castaway," he said. "Get some old clothes. I'll wake her up."

"No," whispered the wife, and she gripped his arm. "Be careful. Let her sleep. See how she lies there like a princess? Surely she is no ordinary guest."

The fisherman weighed these words and scratched his head.

"Hmm," he considered, "it may be so. If she is rich, we must treat her courteously. I shall go and mend my nets; do not disturb her. Call me as soon as she awakes."

But the maiden only slept.

All day the old woman watched her guest. The fisherman took his nets and went to sea, and at sunset when he returned for his beer and bread, the maiden still slept. She did not appear ill; her face was peaceful. But she had not stirred even an inch.

This went beyond the bounds of courtesy. At twilight, the two discussed what they should do.

"Wife, I don't like it. It's unnatural to sleep the way she does. All day she's slumbered in our hut. Suppose she's ill with some terrible disease that will make us just as sick? Suppose she's mad or wanted for some crime? She may be a runaway with a bounty on her head."

The old woman frowned. She did not think the guest was a runaway, nor did she think the girl was ill. She had watched her very carefully all day long. Again, she told her husband how she had found the marvelous pearl, but the fisherman grew angry and shook his head. "Wife, don't speak such nonsense! What does a pearl have to do with this? You should have kept it; pearls can be sold. This stranger is a runaway or a castaway, or else a young wench dishonored by her lover whose family has abandoned her to a miserable fate. Come on. Let's try again. We must wake her."

But the wife held his arm.

"Wait," she implored. "Show some pity."

To and fro, they argued what to do.

At last as the twilight deepened, the fisherman had his way. He shook aside his wife and her complaints, and he turned to his hut determined to awaken the sleeping stranger. When he opened the door to go inside, a pale, blue light shone forth. The light was so strong that it made him blink.

"Wife," he said to the woman angrily, "did you light all our precious candles? What madness made you burn them all at once?"

"Husband, I lit no candle," the woman said.

Suspicious now, the fisherman entered his hut, shielding his eyes as he peered through the narrow entry.

His wife had told the truth. She had lit no candles. The light came from the maiden, who no longer slept. The maiden had risen from her bed of seaweed in the corner of the miserable hut, and now she sat patiently weaving cloth at the old woman's loom.

"Here now, what's the meaning of this?" demanded the fisherman. "Girl, who are you? Step outside."

But the maiden did not speak. Her skin glowed with a cool, silver-blue radiance that illumined the tiny hut but did not warm it. Her light was as bright as a full, midsummer moon. The maiden sat at the loom and wove very skillfully. She was completely naked. The woman's tattered shawl had fallen to the floor. Only the maiden's long black hair concealed her lovely body here and there.

She wove at the loom, and not for a moment did she pause. With practiced, even motions she finished a cloth that the old woman had begun weeks earlier but had left undone. She worked so quickly that her movements were nearly a blur.

"Girl, stop," said the fisherman sternly. "Look at me. Who are you? Where do you come from? What do you want? Who brought you here? Who are your parents?"

But the maiden did not answer. She continued to weave.

At last the fisherman grew angry and raised his voice.

"Girl, stop!"

At these harsh words the maiden abruptly halted. Her light grew dim. She inclined her head sadly, and her expression showed pain, distress, and surprise.

"Look what you've done," hissed the fisherman's wife. "You old fool, you've hurt her feelings. Poor dear! She's alone in the world with no one to help her. How can you be so heartless?"

The woman fetched her shawl and draped it over the maiden's naked shoulders.

"There, there," she said, "my dear one, don't be sad. You're safe in our home. My husband will protect you. Don't mind his silly words. It's all right to use our loom. Work, if it makes you happy! Are you cold? Are you hungry? How did you get here? Are you lost?"

But the maiden said nothing. She sat silently and gazed at the floor.

She began to weep.

"I'm sorry," said the old fisherman.

And truly, he meant that he was.

Husband and wife waited patiently while the maiden shed her tears. At last she stopped. Without wiping her eyes or bothering in any way to adjust the tattered shawl that the old woman had draped on her bare shoulders, she began to weave. Once more, her fingers danced like fairies.

"Wife, what shall we do?" whispered the fisherman.

The old woman did not know.

Perplexed and defeated, the two old people sat down at their only table, and they ate their meager bread.

The maiden did not speak. All night she wove in silence. The fisherman and his wife could not help but watch. Neither of them could sleep. They felt fascinated by her weaving. The cloth that she wove was quickly done. But at once she began again. Her art was masterful. At last, as the eastern horizon brightened, the maiden's hands grew still. Before the sun appeared, she lay down beside her loom on her bed of seaweed and went to sleep.

The fisherman and his wife lay down also. Exhausted, they fell asleep at once and slept until the sun had almost set.

The old woman woke first.

She poked her snoring husband. "Wake up," she whispered. "Pay attention."

Her husband grumbled awake just as the sun passed below the western horizon. As soon as the sun had set, the maiden woke. While asleep, her skin did not glow, but as soon as she awoke she began to shine, though tonight she shone less brightly than the night before. Without a word she rose from her bed of seaweed and took her seat at the loom. Except for a sip of spring water that the old woman fetched in a copper bowl, she refused all food and drink. She neither spoke nor sighed nor indicated anything that might give a clue who she was, why she had come, or how long she might possibly stay. She only wove, and her work was so exquisite that neither the old woman nor the fisherman had ever imagined that human hands could weave such precious cloth. The cloth that she made was finer than priceless silks.

The old woman understood. "Ah, husband," she sighed. "You see how it is. The poor child is enchanted. She has to weave. Look at the magic she can do. This cloth is priceless. Quick, go outside and dig up that pot you buried long ago. Bring me the coins that are in it. I will use them to purchase thread."

"Woman," said the fisherman, "are you mad! That pot is for emergencies. We need those coins for our old age. I've been saving them for thirty years."

"Fool," said his wife, "can't you see your feet unless you trip! This cloth is worth a fortune! Give me all your money; give it now! I shall purchase the cheapest threads. This maiden is the answer to our prayers. She is our angel. God has sent us an angel to make us rich!"

"Ah," said the fisherman slowly, "you may be right." He remembered his many tiresome days upon the sea and the many times his nets had come up slack. "I'll get the pot."

Quickly, he did as his wife had told him to do. He dug up the pot in which he had hidden their meager fortune.

The old woman emptied the pot and clutched the coins tightly.

The next morning, just before sunrise, she hurried to the market and bought as many skeins of cheapest wool as she could afford. Then she hurried home to await the sunset.

Just as before, the maiden woke as the sun passed beneath the western horizon. She at once saw the old woman's gift.

"Ah," she exclaimed delightedly, "you are kind!"

These were the first words she had spoken. Her sudden speech astounded the old couple and made them afraid.

"So you can talk?" they asked with a single voice.

The maiden nodded. In the deepening twilight, it was plain that she no longer shone. The fisherman was forced to light a candle.

"Who are you?" asked the woman. "Are you the angel sent by God to help his poor believers in time of need?"

"No," said the maiden, "I am not."

Those were her only words. Having said them, she sat down at her loom and began to weave. All night she kept busy, pausing only to sip the water that the fisherman fetched from the spring and brought to her in a copper bowl, and at dawn she lay down and went to sleep.

Thus the pattern continued for many nights.

❁ ❁ ❁

Now it so happened that the king of that foreign country had an only child, a prince whose mother had died in childbirth. The prince was a cripple. His left leg was shorter than his right. As an infant, he was frail, often ill with fevers, and physicians were his constant, dear companions.

The king was always mindful of his son. He sent riders to the eight directions to search out healers and cures. Fruits and herbs from distant, exotic climates were fetched for the prince at great expense, and wise men were brought for his education.

One day when the prince was sixteen years of age, a rider came to the palace bearing with him a bolt of cloth. Leaping from his mount, the man ran to the king. "Sire," he exclaimed, "behold what I have found. Cloth of such texture, there is none to surpass it."

The king raised the fabric to the light. The threads were so cunningly woven that they shimmered like gold. He touched the cloth to his cheek and smiled. "Why, it is softer than silk! Where did you get it? Is there more? Come, I must show this to my son."

The prince sat in the garden, hearing his lessons read aloud. He often spent his time there, soothed by the murmur of many fountains. When he saw the splendid cloth, he, too, was delighted and intrigued. He smiled and laughed.

"Father, where did you get it? It is woven sheer as light! Who made such glorious fabric?"

"I, too, would like to know," agreed the king. "The rider says a fishwife sold the cloth. The fishwife's daughter did the work."

For a moment the prince was still, withdrawn to some inner realm of spirit, and his brow creased with thought. "Father," he said at last, "this cloth is rare; it has strange power. Touch it—do you not feel summoned in your heart?"

But the king felt nothing when he touched the splendid cloth; he only admired it for its value and priceless workmanship. He told the prince he would send his men for more.

"No," said the prince, "do not send riders. I want to see this fishwife's daughter. I must meet the maiden who can weave such otherworldly cloth."

Never before had the king heard his son speak so forcefully. Indeed, the prince had never left the palace compound, not even on the high days of festival when the statues of the gods were carried out.

"It is not wise," the king cautioned.

But the prince was determined. Having set his mind at last upon a goal, he would not be contradicted.

And the king, because he loved him, had to agree.

That very day the prince rode forth. A hundred able warriors rode behind him. Each was a leader of men. Each was a peerless fighter, distinguished in mortal combat with seasoned foes. Each bore a banner, armor, and a splendid shield that sparkled in the brilliant sunlight. The iron hooves of their mighty chargers beat upon the ground like peals of thunder and stirred up clouds of dust that were visible to the farthest corners of the realm.

They rode to the western sea. It was night and the moon had risen by the time the host reached the coast. The men had lit torches, and the flames of those many torches danced like a forest set ablaze. Already at a great distance the fisherman and his wife had seen and heard their approach. When the army arrived with their banners snapping, crimson by torchlight, the old couple ran from their home and collapsed in abject terror on the beach.

They made a curious sight, for although they had not been able to remove the strange maiden from her accustomed corner of the hut, they had spent much wealth from the sale of her precious cloth to purchase the most expensive clothes and jewelry. There they cowered on the beach. They looked like two children caught dressed in their parents' finery.

The prince rode forward and stopped. His army halted. "Fisherman, look at me," he commanded. He unfurled the fine cloth that his father had shown him. "Fisherman, is it your daughter who made this? Where is she? Tell me at once!"

A terrible pause ensued in which the only sounds came from the ocean waves. The fisherman trembled. He could not look up. His wife, too, bowed in terrified silence.

"Speak!" the prince commanded.

The poor fisherman dared only point. With trembling finger, he directed the prince toward his hut.

The prince dismounted. At once several warriors leaped to help. "Your Highness, let us carry you! Do not soil your noble feet!" But the prince ordered them back. Alone and unassisted, he limped across the sand to the fisherman's hut and stepped inside.

There the maiden sat weaving, as she did each night from sunset until dawn. She wore a linen shift that the old woman had forced her to put on for the sake of modesty. Her bed of seaweed had been refreshed with kelp and straw. But her ankle was padlocked to a stout chain that the fisherman had secured to a massive anchor. The flesh had begun to discolor where the iron tentacle clenched.

The maiden wove by the light of three candles. Piles of thread and cloth lay strewn across the floor. Bolts of precious cloth lay stacked in a corner of the shack, heaped like goods in a warehouse.

The prince stood still. Amazed, he scarcely breathed. For years he had spent his time alone, confined to his father's palace, with no one for company but his tutors, the courtiers and courtesans, and the king. All that he knew of life he had learned from study, from books that his tutors read to him aloud. Now, as he gazed at the beautiful maiden, he felt transported to a distant realm. She was more glorious than the most glorious courtesans in his father's palace. Her beauty, even in poverty, was unsurpassed. "Who are you?" he asked in wonderment. "Where have you come from? What is your name?"

The maiden scarcely looked at him. Her hands moved swiftly upon the loom. "My name is Aluysha; the loom has summoned you. More than that, you do not need to know."

"Ah," said the prince, "but I do—I must know everything! Are you the daughter of this fisherman? Why do you work in darkness? Does your father compel you to weave?"

The lovely maiden averted her eyes. "My father loves me. I weave because I must. Why do you watch me so closely? Am I so ugly?"

"No," said the prince, "you are not ugly; you are the most beautiful woman I have ever seen! Come with me; leave this hovel. Ride with me to my palace and be my queen!"

The maiden heard these words but showed neither emotion nor surprise. She continued to weave. "No," she said, "it is impossible. You do not know what you ask. Take all the cloth that I have woven; return to your palace. Learn contentment and duty, as I have done. Obey your father, the king."

And she continued to weave. The chain on her ankle rattled angrily. Her fingers danced.

Her words made the prince upset. No one had ever contradicted him. Not even his father could refuse him one of his whims. If any lesser person dared oppose him, that poor misfortunate was exiled, tortured, or burned.

"You refuse because I am deformed!" the prince exclaimed, nodding at his leg. "If I were like other men, you would agree."

"You are the prince," she answered simply, her eyes cast down.

"Then let us marry. You shall be my queen!"

"Ah," sighed the maiden, "I cannot. You do not know me. I cannot marry, not even if you proved your love three times."

"Three times or thirty thousand," swore the prince. "I shall do whatever you want. Speak! I swear I love you. I will love you eternally. Tell me what I must do to possess your heart!"

At these bold words the maiden ceased to weave. She turned from her loom, and her dark eyes keenly searched the prince's face. Her expression became stern, and for a moment queenly. Her tone of voice held ice. "Three things you must do if you would have me: three deeds impossible to mortal men. I do not ask you to do this. I warn you not to try."

"Tell me," said the prince. "I pledge my life."

For a moment the maiden was silent, and the prince shifted nervously under her gaze. "Very well," she said at last, "you must fetch me two things. The first is a flower that blooms on the farthest glaciers of the northland. The flower is very rare. It blooms only at the hour of midnight and only once every twenty-four years. Bring me that flower with the dew still fresh on it petals—this task is the first.

"Second, in the darkest depths of the western ocean lies a jewel. It fell there out of heaven when the moon was created from the earth. Find that jewel and bring it with the flower. That is the second deed, but the third is more difficult yet. The third can only be accomplished when the first two tasks are done. Until that time, the third and greatest task remains a secret. Speak truly, my bold lover; do you now repent your pledge?"

The prince went pale when he heard what the maiden wanted. Yet, he spoke at once in as firm a voice as he could muster.

"I do not repent; my oath has bound me. I shall find these things and win you for my bride."

❁ ❁ ❁

At dawn the prince rode home to his father's palace. He rode in silence, cloaked in thought.

How can I accomplish these two impossible deeds? Such tasks are beyond the strength of any man. What curse binds her to that loom? Is she human, or am I deceived?

At the palace gate, the king greeted him. The king saw at once that the prince was greatly troubled, and when he learned the reason, he, too, became upset. "My son, give up this mad idea. She is only a woman; there are others just as fair."

"Father," said the prince, "you do not understand. I love her. She is the most beautiful woman I have ever seen. There are none who can compare. I love her, and if she cannot be my queen, I shall sicken and die. I must meet her challenge, even if I perish in the attempt. My heart commands me. She is the only woman I will ever love, and I have sworn to have her as my bride."

This answer increased the king's anger, but he saw that the prince could not be swayed. "Very well," he sighed, "you are stubborn and determined with the folly of first love, but I shall help you. My son, this world is vast. Within my realm are men of high renown—magicians whose powers far exceed those of mortal men. These magicians owe me favors; I can summon them."

But the prince demurred.

"I must do this myself. She commanded me."

"Son, do not be an utter fool! Rely on your reason, not your pride. Think it through. How will you climb the northern mountains? How will you plumb the western sea? Only a mage can meet this challenge. Let me summon the magicians to my court."

The prince hesitated. He remembered the western ocean: vast and endless it stretched away. How could he retrieve a single jewel from its bottomless depths? And the mountains, what of them? He recalled how on clear autumn days he caught glimpses of the distant granite peaks. Those peaks were ever white with snow.

"Who are these magicians?" he asked his father. "Are not these tasks too difficult even for them?"

The king only smiled. "My son, the magicians are very strong. What to us may be impossible, *they* can achieve."

Soon, the king's swift messengers flew from the palace. They rode to the eight directions. Within a fortnight the king's summons had been relayed throughout the realm. From forest glen and desert waste, from grotto deep and aerie high, the wizards came. They came to the king's palace and assembled before his throne. Then began a great tournament, for the king demanded that the wizards prove their skills. The king willed that only the strongest and canniest wizard should help his son. Each sorcerer vied with the others, and for days the palace was a scene of wonderment, mayhem, and charms. At its height the tournament raged so fiercely that the sun darkened and the foundations of the palace quaked and heaved.

In the end only three of the wizards remained. Two of these had battled to a draw, but the third survived by cunning. The third wizard had changed himself to a flea at start of the tournament. As a flea, he had hidden on a dog, and there he had slept until the others were exhausted.

❦ ❦ ❦

"Wise men of power," said the king, "it pleases me to accord you greatest honor. You have survived the tournament and proven your skills. For this I shall reward you; for this I ask a boon."

The two wizards who had fought to a draw stood proud as the king addressed them, but the third wizard who had changed into a flea at the start of the grand commotion hunched like a peasant, scratched, and frowned. He was the oldest of the wizards. Unlike the others, who had arrived at the court dressed in their high regalia, this third enchanter wore only a tattered cloak. Barefoot and unkempt, with burrs and dried-up oak leaves in his hair, he looked like the sort of enchanter who knew only one trick well: the sort who made his living conjuring rain or blessing pregnant cows. The other two wizards, whose reputations were very great, ignored this tattered mountebank. They thought that he had cheated in the tournament—for, after all, any wizard might have hidden as a flea.

The king ordered his courtiers to assemble. Then, when all were present and listening, he told them the story of the fisherman's strange daughter, telling how his son, the prince, had fallen deeply in love and explaining how the maiden had posed her impossible demands. His son stood by him as he spoke.

The king finished and challenged the wizards to respond.

"Sire," laughed the first, "you may assume that the flower is yours. I shall change myself to an eagle and fly to the summit of the northern Alps. What skill is required do this? My apprentice could perform such an easy deed!"

The second wizard was just as self-certain. "Is this the reason you have summoned me? Sire, my talents far exceed your crude demands. What child's play it shall be to find that jewel! I shall change myself into a whale and recruit all the fish to be my helpers. Before my colleague has flapped to the northern Alps, you shall have the precious jewel the maid demands."

The king was well pleased to hear this. He smiled upon the wise men and his son. "Go," he said to the wizards. "Fulfill these tasks."

Swirling their midnight capes, the two wizards vanished from the court amid puffs of noxious smoke. The courtiers coughed and applauded, and the king summoned servants to pour the wine. He bowed to the startled prince. "Now, my son, you shall see the extent of my power. The flower and the jewel shall soon be yours."

The prince smiled wanly. Much as he anticipated the wizards' swift return, he felt greatly troubled in his heart. His eyes roamed the room and rested on the third remaining wizard, the one who had hidden as a flea. Squat and gnarled and moody, this third wizard stood in silence amid the gay festivity of the court.

"Father," asked the prince, "and what of him?"

At this question the third wizard approached the throne. Ignoring the guards, he came right to the king's dais.

The king was not pleased to see this unmannerly tramp. He ordered him back, but the old man did not obey. He looked at the prince, who could not avert his eyes. Then, in a voice like sighing wind, the old wizard said: "King and Prince, think well of yet the third and greatest task."

"Seize him!" cried the king, who saw that the old man's words disturbed his son. "He is not a true wizard! He is a cheat!"

"*Cheat*, my lord?" said the wizard. "Well should you know the truth of *that!*"

The king, with a cry of anger, drew his sword and swung at the enchanter's head, but at just that moment the third wizard performed his only trick. With a quick gesture and muttered verse, he shrugged aside his human shape, became a flea, and disappeared.

True to their words, the two mighty wizards soon returned. Within a fortnight the precious jewel and flower were fetched to the prince's hand. At once the prince rode westward to the coast, accompanied by his hundred men at arms. He bore the jewel and flower in a box lined with gold, and yet, though he rode quickly, his heart was as heavy as lead, for he could not forget the third enchanter's words. *But what could I have done?* he asked himself. *Without the help of the wizards I could never have fulfilled these urgent deeds. The maiden is unjust. She sees how I truly love her; yet she is cruel!*

As he neared the fisherman's hut, the prince halted his hundred men. "Stay here," he told them, and he advanced the rest of the distance by himself. Once more he had come at night, and the full moon had risen. Above the ocean's murmur, he could hear the clack of the loom.

The fisherman and his wife ran to greet him, but the prince ignored them. He had no thought for anyone but his love.

Inside, the hut seemed very cramped—far smaller than he had remembered. Only a single candle burned for light, though the moon shone full through the window. The maiden sat weaving and did not turn her head. Her black hair shone like polished lacquer in the moonlight. Even amid the shadows, the prince could see that the cloth she wove was the most gorgeous she had ever made. "I have brought you the flower and the jewel . . ." the prince began, though his voice felt broken and hoarse. His heart beat as fast as a hummingbird's wing.

"Lay them on the table in the moonlight," the maiden said. She did not look up.

The prince put down his burden and stood back. Outside, the waves of the ocean were constant and dull; above that steady monody rose the neighs and nervous stampings of the horses ridden by the prince's hundred men.

The maiden wove quickly, as though she had little time. Twice, as he watched her, the prince began to speak, but his voice felt lost and drowned. He wanted to confess and tell her how it was not he but the wizards who had fetched the flower and the jewel. But he thought: *if she knows the truth she will despise me. It is better to lie than lose my only hope.*

"Ah," said the maiden, "it is done."

Sighing, she put aside her shuttle and stood.

The prince's eyes went wide. Was it only the moonlight that made her face tremble and faintly shine? He could not tell. She appeared so beautiful that the pangs of his desire made him weak. Then, as she came near, he inhaled a marvelous scent. The flower from the mountaintop had opened. The moon shone full upon its crimson petals, and the jewel, close beside it, glimmered bright.

The maiden said nothing. She took a simple teacup and filled it with water freshly dipped from the fisherman's spring. Into the cup she placed the flower and the jewel, then she offered the cup to the prince.

"Two deeds have you accomplished, and yet the third remains," the maiden said. "It is, as I have told you, the most difficult task of all. Take this cup; it is the last of my challenges. The water bears the flower and the jewel. Drink, but know this well: if there is any falsehood in your heart, the water will kill you. Even the smallest lie will strike you dead."

The prince, pale and uncertain, reached for the cup with an awkward, trembling hand.

What shall I do? he thought. *My life is over. By the deeds of my father's wizards, I am condemned. I must confess that I am a liar. The wizards achieved these miracles, not I.*

But the awful fear of losing her restrained him.

Instead, he said: "I have sworn that I love you. I have sworn that your love is more precious to me than life. Whatever lies I harbor in my heart, this much is true: I love you, though it cost me all I am."

And he raised the cup to drink.

But just as the prince made his answer, a wind began to howl. It swirled fiercely upon the cabin, slamming open the flimsy door. The prince stood frozen, the cup raised halfway to his lips. Through the open doorway of the shack, he saw clouds, whiter than snow, blot out the moon and stars. The clouds swirled and billowed, and suddenly they transformed into an army on glistening steeds.

The cloud-born army swept downward toward the beach. At its head, resplendent in pearl-white armor, rode a warrior with flaming hair. Six arms that warrior had, and each arm swung an axe. Great bloody tusks, like those of a boar, arched from his grinning mouth, and his eyes gleamed red as molten iron. About his neck he wore a necklace of clattering human skulls, and his horse breathed smoke and fire and jagged lightning.

The prince's hundred men hurled aside their weapons and fled. They were not pursued. The fierce warrior, whose army now hovered along the waves, reined his horse near the fisherman's meager hut. "Aluysha," he cried, "come out! Your time of exile and penance is at end!" He took a great breath and blew at the tiny cabin, and the walls, which were only sun-bleached planks, scattered like chaff.

Stunned by this tornado, the prince collapsed. The cup he had taken fell from his hand and shattered; the flower and the precious jewel were lost.

But Aluysha stood unmoved. She turned to the fearsome rider. Her dark eyes flashed. "My brother," she said, "be silent. I need not endure your harsh commands!"

The great, cloud-born warrior snarled, and his snarl split the air like thunder. "Aluysha, have you not heard? I have ridden here to fetch you. Would you linger in this foul, polluted land? Our father has forgiven you. Our mother begs and moans for your swift return. Come, Aluysha, away!"

The warrior spurred his ivory steed, riding close as though he meant to strike. But Aluysha raised her arms, and at this gesture, the warrior and his army all fell back. "So, my noisy brother, see what your elder sister yet can do! Keep silent now, the lot of you, or I shall blast you with whirlwinds of sand!"

At once Aluysha's anger stripped the snarling warrior of his evil, monstrous face, and he became a sulking child. "Aluysha!" he muttered spitefully.

Aluysha looked to the sky, to where the moon shone faintly through the clouds. Then, she looked downward, to where her precious teacup had spilled and broken. "Ah, Prince," she said, "this loss is as much my doing as your own. I told you the cup held poison, and yet, it was not true. I spoke to test your valor. Had you sipped that precious drink, you would not have died—for the elixir was such as grants eternal life. Alas, there is no more like it in this world."

"Come, Aluysha," her brother called again. "Have you not yet learned your lesson? Come away now—fly! Return with me to our celestial palace. There you will forget this sordid world."

The prince watched in horror as Aluysha took a step toward the riders above the waves. As she walked, she began to shine.

"Wait!" cried the prince. "Who are you? Where are you going?"

Aluysha turned, gleaming as she spoke. "Dear Prince, I am one of the Immortals who dwell beyond the moon. In my homeland there is no sickness, pain, or death. We dwell in bliss, and yet, for just that reason, I was exiled to your world. I was sent here to do penance for my pride."

"To deceive me!" the prince exclaimed. And at once he regretted his spite, for he saw how his words did wound her. "Wait!" he shouted, but Aluysha shook her head.

With a shrug, she shed the thin dress that the fisherman's wife had given her. Naked and resplendent, she leaped to her brother's silver stallion, shoving the brat aside. "Away!" she commanded, as the imp seized the mane of another mount. Her cry enthused the riders, who blazed like stars.

Just as they turned, Aluysha cast from her hand a spark of heavenly light. It fell to the beach, close to the prince. It was the same blue pearl that the fishwife once had found. "Take it," cried Aluysha, "it is all that I can give you. Dear Prince, you will see me in its depths."

The prince cried out and winced at the blinding light. Shielding his face, he staggered toward the sea.

Aluysha was gone. Gone, too, were the heavenly riders. Their light retreated westward across the waves. Squinting, the prince saw the riders transform their wrathful shapes. No longer an army, they became a flock of cranes.

The snow-white cranes flew upwards, toward clouds that parted as they climbed. Higher and higher the cranes ascended. Their flight grew ever fainter, until at last they disappeared.

❀ ❀ ❀

In later years, the prince became a king. He ruled well and wisely, and yet, he never wed. At times when the moon shone full, he went alone to the heights of his palace to contemplate the jewel, the pearl that Aluysha had left behind. There were nights when he thought he could see her in the depths of that azure gem, though the vision passed as swiftly as a dream.

As for the fisherman, he and his wife returned to the western shore. Patiently, they gathered all the cloth that Aluysha had woven and they sold it for a very great price. "Ah wife," said the fisherman, "now we are truly rich in our old age." His wife only nodded, knowing well what her husband meant.

Long and content were the years those two lived together, married till the ending of their time.

THE CONSOLATION OF PHILOSOPHY

One

All day long the sky had been red. A bad sign. He'd seen this color once before. The river ran red during the summer that had no end. Many people died that year. Some even went mad and frothed at the mouth.

When the river ran red he was still a young man. Just before dawn, the coolest hour, he stripped to the waist and visited *her*. Often he took some ice along—ice he had preserved carefully throughout the day. They never made love while the river ran red, but seeing each other was good, and the ice was good. It reminded him of other worlds.

Sometimes the ice melted before he arrived. Once, a madman tried to steal it. They fought until the madman had a stroke. Then he felt sorry and held ice to the madman's lips. Only after the ice had melted did he continue on his way. That evening, when he saw her, he had to confess. But naturally, she had consoled him.

"Eliot, don't worry. That madman will never die."

These were not his words. They were *hers*. And, like everything else, they were shifting. Some days, they could hardly be found.

One night long ago he'd met an angel. This he was sure of. The angel was pale and serenely smiling. It wore T-shirts and dungarees, and it traveled on a jackass.

Eliot thought this was queer. He'd asked the angel: *are there no horses in heaven?* And the angel answered: *yes, but they are all too precious to ride.*

So Eliot offered the angel his own horse, or even the truck that was used by him alone. But the angel politely refused.

The angel's name was Enoch. Every year when the blueberries were ripe, Enoch descended from heaven in a sphere of light and took up residence in a cave. There he sojourned for about a month, eating berries, taking walks, and fishing.

One day Eliot asked Enoch why no other angels came down from heaven.

"It's my miraculous substance," Enoch told him, thumping his gut. "You see; I never died. God just plucked me up one day to heaven. I've still got my body."

This was true. Eliot had confirmed the allegation by research.[1]

❦ ❦ ❦

Eliot was not an ambitious man. He lived at home with his elderly mother and spent most of his time in the woods. Sometimes, when his mother insisted, he did odd jobs for a neighbor, but he had no strong taste for careers.

"The important thing in life is to be free," Eliot frequently told Enoch when they were fishing or at the cave. "It's not as though I'm a religious man, but I do believe we're set on earth to do something more important than hold a job. A man has got to breathe a bit—expand a little outward."

Whenever Eliot went on this way about his life and worldly ambitions, Enoch told stories about heaven. At first Eliot only listened from politeness. Strange climates and foreign terrains held very little appeal for him. Enoch's descriptions, though passionate and colorful, all seemed slightly irrelevant to things as they were. Eliot appreciated his angelic friend's point of view, but only when Enoch spoke of the mechanical properties of Paradise did Eliot show any real interest. Ideas such as the *Revolution of the Celestial Spheres* intrigued Eliot in respect to their dimensional aspects.[2] Frequently he asked Enoch to explain details of some peculiar motion. Such lectures were absorbed with wide-eyed fascination.

So it was that one cloudless but very humid night in early summer, Eliot had his first Divine Inspiration.

It happened while he and Enoch were drinking beer.

"But what's it like in space, Enoch?" Eliot persisted, pointing upward. "Is space like heaven?"

"Space?" said Enoch. And he slowly scratched his chin. "Hell, no, Eliot. Space and heaven have nothing in common. Space is just a—how shall I say?—an *in-between*. I dread it every time I come here."

"But what's it like? Is it cold? Are there breezes?"

"Breezes!" snorted Enoch. "Hell, Eliot, no. Space is *nothing*. There's nothing there but nothing. Not even *air*."

"Not even air?" said Eliot. And he flapped his hand to demonstrate air's ubiquity.

"No," said Enoch somberly. "Not a bit."

Eliot pondered this metaphysic and drank some beer. He looked at the stars, twinkling.

"Well," he said at last, "if there's no air in space, then that must mean it's a vacuum."

Enoch nodded. He did not dispute.

"Is there air in heaven, Enoch?"

"No," said Enoch. "None."

From this arose the Problem of the Ascent.

Eliot's theory was ingenious. Following the example of Archimedes,[3] a person Eliot had admired from an early age, Eliot postulated that if he could create a vacuum large enough to displace an amount of air equal to his weight, he would rise like an angel to heaven.

To test the validity of this hypothesis in a correct and scientific manner, Eliot decided to abandon home and mother and move into Enoch's cave.

❁ ❁ ❁

A typical attempt at the creation of a vacuum involved the Postulate of the Intermediate Medium. Obtaining a wine barrel from a local vineyard, Eliot and Enoch caulked the seams to make the barrel air and watertight. Then, with Eliot inside the barrel, knees to chest, Enoch submerged the barrel in a pond. When Enoch pushed the sealed end of the flooded barrel to the surface by use of his remarkable angelic strength, atmospheric pressure produced a partial vacuum inside the cask. Eliot starved for air, but he held his breath heroically. Then, before releasing the barrel for its ascent to the heavenly spheres, Enoch quickly tried to clamp on the barrel's bottom, thus sealing Eliot inside.

Unfortunately, despite Enoch's supersensible dexterity with a hammer, Eliot could not hold his breath long enough to complete his translation to the spheres. Three times they tried, and three times Eliot nearly drowned.

By Michaelmas Eliot had decided to abandon the Postulate of the Intermediate Medium for lack of experimental corroboration. He began to work on other devices (such as the construction of a Vacu-centrific Airship[4] that would allow the occupant to breathe as he ascended through the ether), but cold weather and a lack of friends were weakening Eliot's resolve. In October, Enoch returned to heaven in a sphere of light. From then until the first snowfall, Eliot lived alone in his cave and chalked intricate diagrams on the walls.

❁ ❁ ❁

At first, Eliot enjoyed his forest solitude. But as the life around him gradually died and the days shortened, he found himself staying awake most of the time.

Numbed by the cold and by a persistent lack of sustenance, he began to fall into trances. It happened as he studied the diagrams in his cave. One moment he'd be adding a line—the next he'd awaken to find himself in the dirt. Eliot didn't mind starvation, but the trances frightened him. He feared that one day he might never wake up, or else that he might fade quietly into insanity.

Infrequently, Eliot found his solitude interrupted by people from town. They stood with torches and flashlights at the mouth of his narrow cave, and they asked questions about his work. Eliot felt glad for their interest and often explained his scientific theories in copious detail.

One day a more disagreeable visitor arrived.

It was his aunt.

Eliot's aunt spent several hours ridiculing Eliot's ambitions and praying for the salvation of his soul. When that didn't work, she shamed him for neglecting his poor, arthritic mother.

Normally Eliot chased away anyone as annoying as his aunt, but this time he felt a certain moral obligation to listen. The cave had awakened his conscience. [5]

After his aunt went away, Eliot sighed and stared at his diagrams wistfully. They no longer made much sense. [6]

❦ ❦ ❦

That night, as he gathered firewood in the forest, Eliot fell into a trance. When he awoke the next morning, he was covered with fresh snow. Instead of standing up, he pretended that his body was frozen to the ground, which indeed it nearly was.

Everything seemed transfigured. Not a single foot or paw print broke the silent white. Lying on his back, he stared up through the barren tree limbs and into the crystal perfection of the sky.

Later, instead of returning to his diagrams, Eliot left the trail to his grotto undisturbed and slogged through the snowy wilderness back to town.

❦ ❦ ❦

Adjusting to civilized life was difficult. Children ridiculed him, and dogs howled when he sauntered past. His embittered, arthritic mother—never overly inclined to conversation—often refused to acknowledge him at all. Whenever she wanted something, she pointed and looked grim.

Resolved to atone for his hermetic existence, Eliot accepted such treatment stoically. He gradually regained his health and presence of mind, and as soon as possible he took a job with the Road Department. It was the first available position he could find. The men he worked with were friendlier than the people in town. They enjoyed hearing about Enoch, and they laughed whenever Eliot told his story of the Ascent.

Eliot's co-workers in the Road Department helped to socialize him. By spring, dogs and children left him alone. Neighbors began to describe him a pleasant albeit eccentric young man who worked hard all day to support his saintly mother.

❦ ❦ ❦

Like all young men taking first steps toward a new career, Eliot found his job with the Road Department very time consuming and tedious in the early years. He now had very few pastimes. He helped his crippled mother around the house, did repairs and yard work, and when summer came, went fishing. Working for the Road Department was a good way to spend one's time, Eliot reasoned, but it wasn't very satisfying. He kept at it because he knew his job by heart. Once they tried to promote him, but he refused. He asked instead that they give him more time off to go fishing.

❦ ❦ ❦

Thus it came to pass that on the first day of blueberry season Eliot found another fisherman by his pond. It was Enoch.

"Hello, Enoch," said Eliot. "How you been?"

Enoch shook his friend's hand.

"Good to see you, Eliot," said the angel. "I'm okay. Have you given up on going to heaven?"

"I guess so," said Eliot. "I just don't have the time. A man's got to be responsible sooner or later. Living in the cave was nice, but it wasn't very productive."

Enoch nodded.

Although the two friends fished for the rest of the afternoon, Eliot never became too enthusiastic over anything that was said. By evening Eliot had nothing to show for his efforts, whereas Enoch had caught a large catfish.[7] This was embarrassing, since, being an angel, Enoch could fish without bait. In order not to irritate his friend, Enoch invited Eliot back to the cave to share his food and beer.

Eliot sighed.

"Boy, I used to miss those summer evenings at the cave. Sometimes during winter, I'd get so lonely to be back there, I'd do almost anything to get away. But I don't really feel that way any more. I'd like to go Enoch, but tomorrow's work."

Enoch frowned. He put a friendly arm on Eliot's back.

"Going to heaven was a crazy idea, Eliot. Don't worry; you haven't missed much."

"No, no, it isn't that."

"Then what? Your job? Your mother?"

"No, no . . . None of that . . . I'm just out of sorts . . ."

Not the words but the tone of this confession touched the heart of the Immortal.

That night, as Eliot walked home from the cave back to town, he noticed people staring at him through their blinds. Two dogs walked behind him with their tails between their legs. And children ran from him crying.

When Eliot reached his house, his aunt came running outside. She hugged Eliot to her bosom.

"Oh Eliot! Your mother loved you!"

Eliot's aunt had never displayed such intimate physical contact, so Eliot quickly concluded that something was wrong. He shook himself free and entered his home. Inside, he saw a bunch of neighbors. Each looked grim. Eliot smiled nervously, and several of the more delicate females broke into sobs. A gray-haired man in a gray banker's suit with a gray silk handkerchief in the pocket came forward and patted Eliot's hand. He took out a silver pocket watch and flipped it open.

"Huh," said Eliot.

The gray man nodded. He took Eliot by the hand and led him through the crowd of weeping neighbors.

The women keened.

Eliot and the banker went into Eliot's mother's bedroom where all the shades were drawn.

"You're a brave lad," the gray man told him.

Eliot looked at his mother's bed. A large undistinguished lump that Eliot surmised to be his mother's body lay covered with a rosy sheet.

"Heart failure," the gray man told him.

It was the end.

Later that evening, as Eliot sat on the front porch and ate the catfish that Enoch had given him earlier that day, a young woman whom he had never seen before walked up the path to his house.

"Hello, Eliot. My name is June."

June Regis was the daughter of May Regis, a close friend of Eliot's dear, departed mother.

"Ma's dead," Eliot told her.

June nodded. She understood.

Two

Life was easier for Eliot with his mother dead. Because she had left a will directing that her house, all her possessions, and the not inconsiderable profit that had accrued from a life-long discipline of investing in blue chip stocks be liquidated and the entire proceeds donated to the Church,[8] Eliot found that he had no inheritance and could break cleanly from his past. Homeless, he moved to the other side of town, took a promotion, and proposed to June.

June accepted, and they were wed.

Eliot's marriage was magical—not because it had occurred without effort, but because it maintained itself without the use of speech.

Eliot now worked ten hours each day overseeing the construction of a bypass turnpike. At night he came home at a regular hour, ate the dinner that June had prepared for him, and promptly went to bed. In the gray, half-conscious moments before sleep, he considered what having a wife could possibly mean. Only with the warm dark length of June's body beside him did he realize he was wed. Thoughts then came to mind—but they were naked, without the cloak of words. He could express himself only through movement: by turning in such a way, by moving a muscle here, by gliding the hand so. Yet, this was enough. June in turn made movements that were answers.

Throughout winter, whenever the memory of Enoch crossed Eliot's mind, he stopped what he was doing and stared at his feet in perplexity. If anything, Eliot now desired to lead a decent life. The time spent with Enoch seemed like lapses of discretion, embarrassing to recall.

But sometimes, after a particularly hard day of work, Eliot turned to June and saw another face. There, illusively merging with her sleepy lips and eyes, were Enoch's features. Eliot observed this with fascination, if not despair. Often after such hallucinations he could not return to sleep. He would instead stand by the window and watch the falling snow. He gazed at the sky for messages and occasionally felt his pulse.

June did not mind. Although she believed in Enoch, she did not believe in miracles. Eliot sometimes wondered why she had married him at all.

She always awoke with Eliot. If the sun were shining brightly she would kiss him enthusiastically before she dressed and say: "Oh, Eliot, this day will be fine!" Or, if instead it rained, she threw a pillow over her head and shivered. Breakfast was served like a ritual. Without it, Eliot could not approach the day.

By performing such duties with dedication and regularity, June created an aura of plenitude about her husband's life. Eliot seldom had to wonder what she thought. No topic or activity occurred without due precedent.

"I baked today, Eliot," June might say at dinner. "You can have fresh bread for your sandwiches."

"That's swell, June. You'll fatten me up yet."

Or:

"You know, June, we started blasting today. I set off a load after lunch. Not really an explosion, more like a thump or a cracking. Afterwards we dig out the rock. We could go faster, but you know how loose those ledges are. We can't risk a slide."

"Are you afraid?" June always asked him.

"Nah, it's all pretty safe. I know where the rocks are, how they're packed and how they'll break. A little at a time and pretty soon you've moved a mountain! Good soup, June. I ought to quit, but give me more."

Only one old habit carried over into Eliot's marriage. Fishing.

Barely had the last snow turned to mud when Eliot began to trek about in search of "holes." Such activity worried June. She remembered the old rumors—they described a half-mad Eliot who took to the woods and grottoes, abandoning family and friends. The Eliot she knew was nothing like that, and she feared the re-emergence of the past. Although Eliot had mentioned that period of his life many times, he always did so with a detachment that June did not trust. She could tell by the tone of his voice that he didn't expect to be understood and therefore said less than he meant.

June's sister, who observed Eliot with an objectivity June could not hope to muster, attempted to clarify matters somewhat.

"He's just a boy. You must indulge him," she said to June.

"But Veronica, he's so stubborn!"

"Well after all, he's only fishing."

Eventually June conceded that her husband would not change his ways. As spring progressed, she even was tempted to accompany him. Encouraged by this acceptance, Eliot began to teach her about fly rods, baits, and casting. Soon they discovered that by cultivating an interest in fishing they could communicate in a way previously impossible. Where before the ties between them had been evocative and wordless, they now spent hours discussing tackle and bait.[9]

Eliot was so gratified by June's interest that in early summer he arranged a fishing trip to Canada. Because he had been with the Road Department for several years, he was entitled to ten days off. June and Eliot planned to leave as soon as the blasting that Eliot supervised was done.

Then, on the last day of work, Eliot did not come home for dinner. June waited as long as possible and finally ate by herself. She was just tidying up the dishes when a group of Eliot's co-workers arrived at the back door. They supported Eliot tensely and soberly between them. They were all encrusted with dirt.

"Accident," one of the men explained. "Explosion. No one hurt."

Eliot's battered appearance contradicted the man's report. June seized her husband's hand.

Immediately she felt repelled.

"What happened?" she demanded.

"Blasting. Eliot knows."

Saying no more, the men put Eliot on the kitchen table and walked backwards out of the room. June was too frightened to ask them any more questions. She watched them retreat until at last they disappeared into the night.

"Asses," said Eliot suddenly. His voice was devoid of all emotion, judgment, or surprise.

"Eliot, dear, what happened?" June exclaimed.

Eliot paused and looked at her inquisitively.

"Can you hear me?" he asked her.

"Yes, of course."

"What am I saying?"

June waited.

"Well?"

"Huh?"

"What did I say?"

"Nothing, Eliot. You didn't say *anything*."

June started to cry. She grabbed her husband's hand, but he shook himself free and walked away.

❁ ❁ ❁

The next morning Eliot looked no worse for the wear. He rose as usual, ate breakfast as usual, read the paper as usual, but remained at the kitchen table long after the meal was done. He amused himself with a rubber band until June at last became angry and demanded an explanation.

"I quit," said Eliot, without reproach or malice. "I just can't work with those people anymore."

This made no sense. June demanded a better answer.

"Well," said Eliot, "I don't know what's all that difficult to understand. I just can't work with those people any longer. They're incompetent. They're asses. I quit."

And without another word, Eliot rose leisurely from the table, put on his fishing hat, and strolled out of the house.

❁ ❁ ❁

For June, the sentence that Eliot spoke to her that morning was the last complete sentence she was to hear from her husband for many years.

As for the facts of that fateful accident, these she eventually had to assemble from the wives of Eliot's co-workers, who knew what had happened from their men.

The gist of the matter was this:

For some reason Eliot's blasting orders were misunderstood by the assistant whose job it was to place the explosive charge. The resulting detonation was too great. Several workers were bruised, equipment was damaged, and an old dray horse died of cardiac arrest. Eliot was outraged by the error. He attacked his assistant with a crowbar and nearly broke the poor man's head. Three of the road crew had to sit on him to calm him down. Some people later argued that the explosion had damaged Eliot's brain. No medical tests were forthcoming. The event remains a mystery to this day.

June tried many times to hear a version of this story from her husband. But Eliot only smiled and shrugged complacently. He had become a veritable sphinx.[10] Eliot's and June's marriage returned to that state of speechlessness that had characterized their days of honeymoon, but without a happy outcome in sight. Although this state of affairs seemed congenial to her husband, the situation played on June's nerves and caused her to chain smoke.

But June was not the only one to whom Eliot never spoke. His silence was so adamantine that rumors spread suggesting that the explosion had made him deaf, or that he secretly brooded on some terrible plot of revenge.[11]

June found it hard to deny such rumors. Although she remained a stoic helpmate, she found her martyrdom increasingly difficult to bear. She began to hear voices, and over time she cultivated habits of extreme attentiveness so that she could write down whatever directives these Masters of Interiority deigned to convey.

Eliot didn't fuss about June's dilemma. He fished as much as he liked, whenever he felt like it. Jobs, he had concluded, were over-rated. He harbored no grudge and did not feel wronged—by world, by wife, or fellow man. June and he had saved enough money to support themselves for several months, so Eliot saw no reason to be productive. He abided in silence because in truth he had nothing to say.

Three

In summer, as soon as the first blueberries appeared, Eliot began to keep his eyes open for the angel Enoch. When at last the blueberries were ripe, Enoch descended from heaven in a sphere of light and took up residence in the cave. Enoch was not at all surprised by the changes in Eliot's life, since as an angel he had more or less foreseen them. Yet, he denied all culpability for the events.

"Don't blame your troubles on me," Enoch protested. "I only suggested a direction. You're the one who decided what to do."

Although Eliot suspected that Enoch had done more than merely suggest, he kept quiet for the sake of friendship.

When June learned that Enoch had returned to the cave, her worries changed to anger and she threatened to move out. She distrusted the angel's intentions; she feared that the Immortal had designs on her husband's life.

The result was insomnia. Every night while Eliot was at the cave, June paced up and down the empty corridors of her mind until despair and exhaustion overcame her.

At last, her very worst fears were confirmed.

Although Eliot sincerely believed that he had reconciled himself to silence, beneath his hermit's calm brooded a tension of which he was wholly unaware. This tension soon revealed itself as his Second Divine Inspiration.

"One thing that really annoys me, Enoch," said Eliot one night, "is the stupidity of people in general. You know what I mean?" (He had begun to talk to the angel, if not to June.)

Enoch sat playing with the campfire. When he heard Eliot's question, he dropped the coals.

"It's not that I claim to be perfect," Eliot said, "but at least I do my best."

"Yeah," nodded Enoch. "Life can be aggravating."

"Like for instance," said Eliot, "that incident at work. You can tell someone something twenty times—what good does it do? A man's damn lucky if he's ever understood by anyone."

"In heaven, we don't really have that problem," the angel said.

"What do you mean you don't have that problem in heaven?"

"It's due to the miraculous nature of the place. We're fed off divine love. Divine love permeates us so completely that we're all on the same page, more or less. And the way I figure it, the reason those old humans like Methuselah[12] lived so long was because humans were once so close to the first creation. In those days, we were all just pickled in God's Love. Gradually, the juice just seeped away. Now you're dried out. You humans, I mean. On earth, if you get my meaning."

Eliot pondered these words for a very long time. He found the Immortal's metaphors confusing.

"The same with marriage," he answered finally.

"Huh," said Enoch sagely. "It's the Fall."[13]

When June awoke the next morning, she found a note beside her on the bed. Written in purple crayon, the note said:

"June. Last night while returning home from the cave, I was taken with a vision. I know that you will be angry, but the explanation is very clear. I CANNOT STAND THE CONFUSION ANY LONGER. My decision is the only one possible. Please don't be mad. I took most of the food, but there is money on the counter. I have considered my action carefully. I know I am right. I will love you forever. Eliot."

June read this note and cried.

Four

Shortly after receiving Eliot's note, June left home and moved in with her sister, Veronica. Eliot became a scientist. And since the house of his marriage now stood empty, he decided to perform his experiments there.

He soon constructed a laboratory and began work on what the learned later called Organic Alchemy.[14]

The goal of these endeavors was the extraction of Primal Love[15] from food.

To most people, Eliot's "science" seemed no more than an obsession with diet. The theory, however, was far more elegant and ingeniously complex.

Eliot postulated that all life had as its basic unit of being a substance he termed the Generatus.[16] Generatus had been created directly by God. Life in all its complexity was a result of permutations of the Generatus; these permutations[17] were caused by the induction of Vitalia,[18] an energy whose origin Eliot's theory did not conclusively explain. To avoid reductive calculations, Eliot postulated a constant to prove mathematically that Vitalia was derived from Primal Love. Vitalia manifested on several levels of potency that Eliot termed V_1, V_2, V_3, etc. for simplicity's sake. Whereas all life had Generatus in common, the level of Vitalia differed from creature to creature and even from human being to human being. One's level of Vitalia determined the way one viewed the world. Whereas the Vitalia level in a man of genius might range as high as 33.333 on the VG scale, in an idiot the Vitalia level might sink as low as -08.88. Since genius and idiocy had the same Generatus in common, Eliot further reasoned that only the disparate levels of Vitalia sowed confusion and inequality among men. From this "Copernican Turn®"[19] he concluded that by extracting the Generatus and refining it to a common level of Vitalia, one could, by means of a purified VG diet, eventually cultivate the same level of Vitalia in all men. Spontaneous communication and universal peace would necessarily occur, since the common state of Vitalia is bliss and the consequent state of substance is similitude.[20]

When Eliot announced his theory to Enoch, the angel frowned.

"Alchemy is a mortal sin, Eliot. I cannot sanction such endeavors."

"What do you mean it's a sin?" Eliot protested.

"It is a sin of godly pride. It is the worshipping of intellect as godhead. Such ambition will bring you misery."

This was not at all the response that Eliot had foreseen. He thought his idea was brilliant. What could be more in the service of piety than an attempt to establish perfect, ecumenical communion among all human beings—and animals, too. Enoch's warning seemed petty, suspiciously Catholic, and overdone.

"I warn you, Eliot," glowered the angel. "Besides," he shrugged, "it's all such obvious nonsense. Let's go fishing."

But this last remark seemed obvious spite.

Although Eliot loved Enoch dearly, he felt too strongly compelled by his daemon to follow the angel's advice. The prospect of establishing communion between all human beings (and animals, too) seemed more important and noteworthy than a concern for mere personal welfare.

"I can't give it up, Enoch," Eliot complained. "You don't understand what this means to me. Think of it—to extract the Primal Love!"

"You'll fail, Eliot," said Enoch somberly. "You will never understand your success."

❀ ❀ ❀

That summer was a time of hardship for Eliot. Not only did Enoch abandon him, the town was much less willing to excuse his queer behavior in the name research. Instead of observing him with condescending smiles, they spoke of him maliciously and called him names. Often their children tormented him and threw rotten apples at his home.

For Eliot, this scorn was especially unfortunate and ill timed. For, in order to perform his experiments successfully, he needed another person to share his diet. When June refused, he turned to the townsfolk. Every afternoon he stood on a street corner and accosted whomever went by.

After weeks of unsuccessful solicitation, Eliot was forced to buy a dog. For nearly two months the dog and Eliot shared a common diet and routine. Although the dog eventually died, Eliot was encouraged. Before expiring, the dog proved increasingly sympathetic and wagged his tail whenever Eliot came near. Eliot took this as confirmation that his theory was essentially sound, and he tried once more to convince his wife to join him.

❀ ❀ ❀

June was not around when Eliot came to call.
This was just as well, since Eliot looked quite dismasted by research.
Veronica, June's sister, met him instead. She was repulsed.
"Eliot!" Veronica exclaimed. "You look like hell."
"Dog's dead. Where's June?"
"June's gone, Eliot. Go away. She doesn't want you. Give up your crazy idea."
"Idea not crazy!" Eliot barked.
And then he fell down.

Years later, when people spoke of Eliot, they ignored his dealings with angels and discussed only his time with Veronica. When their grandchildren were told the story of Father Eliot, they never asked to see the Cave of Enoch or the Organic Laboratory in the House of Love—they were interested only in how the Great Ones met.

Some people suggest that Veronica knew what destiny bound their lives from the moment she first saw her future consort. These people argue that Eliot's visit to Veronica was foreordained. They ignore the fact that June was living with Veronica at the time, for in their eyes June functions only as the means by which Eliot is at last united with his true love.

Such ideas flirt with idolatry.

For, as Eliot fainted at Veronica's feet, he had no idea that when he awakened three days later his life would be transformed. Nor did he realize that the vision of Primal Love that had sustained him during his period of scientific research would vanish during his coma. Even his remembrance of his former life would be lost. Eliot opened his eyes on an unrecognized world, on sensations as traumatic as childbirth—a disordered, kaleidoscopic whirl of mere perception. He whimpered softly, mewed, or tried to sleep. Never did he consider (for he could not) that the bed he lay upon was Veronica's or that only her maternal instincts kept him alive.

Whether Veronica fully cognized the extent of Eliot's pain is hard to say. She allowed him to remain with her when June refused—so perhaps that says enough. Or perhaps, as some suggest, this merely indicates her indifference to circumstance, opinion, and public life. Certainly June could not understand her younger sister's ways. The blood tie that bound them explained nothing. Like Martha facing Mary, June misunderstood. More than common ancestry, June and her sister Veronica had Eliot to unite them. Yet, even *he* seemed more excuse than justification.

If, as theologians have argued, Eliot's "sins" broke the order of nature, then his time with Veronica might be termed unnatural and the incident held suspect. Yet, the experience was undoubtedly real, given the sheer weight of its facticity—

if only that. Too many people have suffered for us to deny its truth. The "crime," if any was committed, was unpremeditated—by Nature or by Man. This is how the town came to view the situation and how they eventually forgave it. Only this can explain the malignancy of Eliot's innocence or the rebirth that was not a renewal, merely event.

Slowly Eliot's memories returned. Like stars appearing through the fog, he began to glimpse a universe he had abjured. He relived his entire life, going backwards. Feeling followed feeling, hurt followed hurt, in a broken, disjointed sequence, or so it seemed.

Veronica observed this recherché with cautious albeit skeptical fascination.

"I often find Eliot weeping," she wrote in her diary, a journal she had kept since her earliest years. "No doubt the things he imagines are very cruel. He is returning to life at a terrible pace. I am intrigued by the pain of his expressions. Like a child, he has no secrets. I could destroy him, if I liked."

And later, when Eliot had regained his past and even talked now and then of daily affairs, she wrote:

"Eliot has rediscovered speech. As yet, there is only music. He sings a great deal, as though trying to anchor himself to life. Yesterday, he sang the song of breakfast. We had poached eggs. Today, he sang the song of the mouse. There is nothing I can say to him—how very strange! June said it was his self-certainty that hurt so much. But she is wrong. It is not self-certainty—but naiveté."

And even later:

"When I looked in on Eliot this morning he was gone. His boots were on the rack, but his clothes were missing. I saw June, but he was not there. Perhaps he will kill himself. June says she cannot tolerate his silence. She says she will move away. I cannot console her. *L'amour*..."

But then:

"This evening, Eliot returned. I found him in the kitchen. He looked at me coldly as though appraising me for the very first time. Perhaps he thought I'd pity him. I did not. I told him he cannot sleep here any longer. He shrugged, as if to say—what can possibly matter? My, but does he not have a great Russian soul!!! When he spoke tonight, his words had signification. He said: 'One thing you must realize, Veronica, is that I have absolutely no regrets about my life.' I told him he's an ass. I will not feed him. He'll have to work."

Eliot readily obeyed Veronica—not because he respected her, but because he felt a great indifference toward his fate.

A curious event had occurred during the time of his disappearance. While walking toward the forest, he had met himself in reverse.

His self, the other Eliot, approached him on foot. The other wore shoes. It was the only observed difference he could recall.

As the other Eliot passed, the true Eliot noticed that the other Eliot smiled. The true Eliot had just decided to pursue the other Eliot when the true Eliot noticed yet a third Eliot walking out of the barbershop down the street. The two untrue Eliots walked straight at one another in reverse. As soon as they collided, they disappeared.

At this moment, the true Eliot felt like someone was tickling him all over and inside out. He fell to the ground and laughed until a crowd gathered in curiosity.

"It's Eliot," one of them whispered.

"Why do you hate us?" someone asked.

"Why don't you die and leave us alone?"

Eliot did not hear what else they said because he felt distracted by something strange. As he looked at the hostile crowd, he noticed that everyone's skin was chapped and parched, as though the flesh had been severely sunburned. Although the day was cool and overcast, the bystanders were sweating profusely.

"I'm sorry," said Eliot. "Please excuse me. I am feeling a bit confused."

As he started to rise, the people turned away and went on about their business. When he approached one of them, the person smiled and then politely inquired about his health.

This experience so unnerved Eliot that he returned to Veronica straight away.

※ ※ ※

That year spring brought many disturbing changes to Eliot's town. Almost as a prefiguration of the summer to come, the cedars turned red and the daffodils bloomed in that color. Such transfigurations signified to Eliot the profundity of the change within himself. The world and his thoughts were congruent. Torn apart during his period of illness, his life had been remade as a Testament of Love. In place of his plan to reach heaven, in place of Organic Alchemy, with the same Promethean genius that had willed the birth of miracles, Eliot envisioned a love for Veronica that was as pure and timeless as Plato's eternal forms.[21] He loved her ideally throughout winter, spring, and the long eternity of the summer later to come. He loved her without cause, encouragement, or doubt. He loved her even though she never allowed him to re-enter her bedroom for fear that this trespass would give their love a sanctity that even the friendliest gods could not accept. He loved her mortally, then, and in pursuit, as though motion were the soul of love. And he paused only to consider their child.

When the child was conceived the river turned red at the start of the summer that had no end. Sustained by their all-consuming passion, Eliot and Veronica could endure that wretched season rather well. Death and despair came to others.

Like a great red wound or the uncoiling snake of time, the river flowed painfully all summer. People dreaded falling asleep, for sleep no longer refreshed them. Upon awakening from fitful slumber, they found that their lives had grown even hotter, if not strange.

The only relief came from ice, but the desire for ice brought madness and turned many into beasts. The weak lost their minds entirely. Like those in a season of plague in ages past, they fled the town and roamed the countryside *solitaire*. Sometimes they attacked old farmers, but usually they ran at the sight of any human. If they could not be trapped, they were shot.

Such violence upset Veronica. Although she could not blame herself, she nevertheless felt implicated. She once confessed to Eliot her fears.
"When I leave you, Eliot, you must make restitution for this pain. I know that you are not guilty and that what you can do is not important in respect to all that's been done, but the mind demands that one soul bow to consequences still forever beyond its control and accept the inevitable truth of its disasters."
Veronica took most of her sentences from foreign novels or complex books. When Eliot heard her, although he had no idea what she meant, he nonetheless felt unsettled. He decided that night to visit June.

June looked at him through the window of her bedroom, but she made no sign for him to enter, and he could not.
"Eliot," she said.
"I'm a father," Eliot told her. "Let me in."
June gazed beyond him toward the fields.
"The summer will end. The nights will be cool. We can sleep. There will be stars."
"Let me in," he repeated.
June shrugged. She said nothing else.

Afterwards Eliot could not return to Veronica's home, but Veronica, wisely, had expected this. She awaited motherhood with a certain virginal pride. She could tolerate the heat. The heat passed through her. She knew that Eliot would tremble when it was done.
Day in, day out, Veronica walked through her house and considered what message she should leave her eternal lover. She leafed through her books and read various passages of prose aloud. When she heard a phrase she liked, she underlined it or cut it out, assembling the scraps into a narrative stitched like a quilt.
At last, she receded into legend.[22]

Five

As soon as the day awakened him, Eliot rose and built a fire in the cave. He bowed to the sun and then got on with business. First, he suspended a battered, blackened pot about the campfire; second, he warmed the goat's milk that he had kept cooling in the stream over night. His infant son, James Eliot, often cried in the wee morning hours, but Eliot had grown used to this over time, and he talked to James Eliot as he performed his morning chores.

The summer had ended at last. The child, James Eliot, would not remember the weight of that unbearable heat. The insufferable days, the scarlet flowers, the river that ran red as an open wound—these he would know only as the stuff of legend.

James Eliot drew his first breath in autumn. The trees did not change color that year; the leaves merely dropped from exhaustion. This, too, James Eliot would not recall; his soul was a blank slate. Though the air he breathed was cool, he knew it no other temperature. It might be eternally so.

Every morning Eliot explained the ways of nature to his son. Sometimes he took a stick and drew diagrams in the dirt. He could not bring James Eliot too close to these intricate drawings because the tiny, excited legs often marred the careful lines.

"One thing I want you to remember, James Eliot, is that things go around each other," Eliot said. "The circle, or rather the spiral, is the fundamental motion of nature. You can see this is so by examining my illustration. Let us posit this rock as the sun. Around this rock I am drawing spirals. These, my son, exemplify what one day you will contemplate as Art."

Perhaps such explanations were premature, given the tender age of James Eliot, infant. But Father Eliot feared that all too soon the town would claim his son. To forestall this event, Eliot wrote several letters to June, and he pleaded for her to accept him—or at least to fulfill a role as surrogate mother, on her sister's behalf. But June would not.

Perhaps Eliot suspected (even during those tender months in the cave) that he would forfeit his humanity to legend. He had confessed this anxiety in imagination to June several times. Every morning he practiced this confession on his son.

"I am stepping out of life. Yesterday, when some townspeople came to the cave, they looked at me fearfully, almost piously. When I spoke to them, they cowered, as though my voice were too great for them to bear. Perhaps I am demonic. I am more afraid than I have ever been. If you cannot accept me, at least adopt my son."

But June remained silent. As soon as she learned that Eliot had left town for the forest cave, she took a can of kerosene and set fire to Veronica's home. Although the fire department soon extinguished the feeble blaze, June had had her revenge. As the hoses quenched the flames, June cried and laughed simultaneously. Afterwards, when she received Eliot's testament, she tore it up. She hid the pieces for safekeeping, but later forgot where they were. Years and years later, when James Eliot discovered those scraps and re-assembled them as a scroll, June met his inquisitions with a shrug.

"Of course it's from your father," June told him. "Read it. I never could."

James Eliot read the testament carefully, but despite his zeal to understand, he could find no meaning in the writing.

June sighed. She said nothing. She seldom did.

Quietly, with stoic pride, she took the scroll and burned it.[23]

Some say that this mystery drove James Eliot mad. Whatever the cause, as James Eliot entered his mature years, he became cynical and superstitious, averse to society, and prone to an extreme distrust of progressive ideas.

While many people publicly praised James Eliot's traditional attitudes and thrifty ways, few people liked him. Instead, they spoke furtively among themselves of the time that James Eliot as a teenager was carried kicking and screaming by members of his football team to a clearing within haling distance of Old Eliot's fabled cave. This was James Eliot's first adult vision of that dark, moss-grown abyss. For months it reappeared in his nightmares.

Such fascination was not extraordinary, by any means. James Eliot's contemporaries had all undergone such initiations in their youth. Although they all denied a lasting impact, no one ever approached the cave alone or spoke of its inhabitant after sunset.

Only June might have spared James Eliot his grief or pardoned the town for guilt it had only imagined. Yet, June's silence was inviolate. Whether she suffered at all in the last years of her life—or, like James Eliot, found some asylum in religion—cannot be ascertained. June's death was outwardly calm. She died sitting up while sipping a tea she had brewed for many years.

Epilogue

When Eliot considered the years ahead, he did not think as persons such as you or I are accustomed to lay our plans—he thought of what he did not want to do. He did not want to be reborn. He thought about this often in the afternoon in the cave as he watched the mid-winter sunlight through the trees. When at last he was no longer Eliot but a hoary Iron John with a long, thistly beard, he still refused the future. The people from town (those few) who then came to see him were given the same advice he had given his son.

"A man doesn't talk to a tree, does he, James Eliot? If a man could talk to a tree, what would be the advantage to being human?"

Thoughts such as these were difficult, and he suffered beneath their weight. But without such unanswered questions, who knows what strange illusions might have claimed him? Already his perceptions were blurred with heavenly scenes. When he looked at the queer, childish drawings on the walls of his hallowed cave, he could not remember who had drawn them, although it was he. When he tried, his mind became dazed.

Recurrently, he had visions of Veronica, but never June. When, in the last years of his fabled life, the woods and the cave disappeared and he moved within timeless space, his memory of Veronica still retained its present tense. It was all he could not reconcile. She had become his lasting Myth.

Between such visions, he maintained an endless prayer. Until one day, as the blueberries ripened, the angel known as Enoch recalled him from his cave to fields of bliss.

Endnotes

[1] "The Book of Enoch: One of the non-canonized books of the Bible from ancient scripts and the Dead Sea Scrolls. This is a selection of chapters from the book of **Enoch** pertaining to Angels and the corruption of mankind. It is by no means a complete rendering. Here is a website <*http://www.ancienttexts.org/library/enoch/index.html*> for those who want a complete rendering. These writings give greater insight into the biblical books of Genesis, and more clearly defines the nature of the past relationship of mankind with extraterrestrial beings. Enoch was the great-great grandfather of Noah. As the Bible states, 'Enoch walked with God: and he was not; for God took him'" (Larry A. Wright, "The Book of Enoch," *Prophecy and Earth Changes: Dedicated to the Divine Plan and the Prophecies of Jesus Christ* 2006 <*http://wrightworld.net/enoch.htm*>).

[2] "When it came to conceptualizing the universe, the medieval world borrowed its knowledge from the Egyptian geographer and astronomer **Claudius Ptolemy** (<*http://www-groups.dcs.st-and.ac.uk/~history/Mathematicians/Ptolemy.html*>). The Ptolemaic System put the stars on a fixed sphere around the earth. At the center was an object about which nine concentric spheres were situated. This object was the earth. Beyond the earth, its position fixed, were the Moon, Sun, Mercury, Venus, Mars, Jupiter, Saturn and then the stars, and finally, the Prime Mover, the First Cause, God" (Steven Kreis, "Lecture 10: The Scientific Revolution, 1543-1600," *The History Guide: revolutionizing education in the spirit of Socratic wisdom* 8 February 2006 <*http://www.historyguide.org/earlymod/lecture10c.html*>).

3   **Archimedes of Syracuse** (287-212 B.C.): "Archimedes, the greatest mathematician of the ancient world and the greatest mathematical genius in Europe until Newton, was born, lived and died in the Greek city-state of Syracuse, in Sicily. He was the son of an astronomer called **Phidias** (<http://en.wikipedia.org/wiki/Phidias>) and was closely associated with (and possibly related to) the city's ruler, **Hieron II** (<http://es.wikipedia.org/wiki/Hier%C3%B3n_II>). He studied at Alexandria, in Egypt, where he met Euclid's successors Eratosthenes and Dositheus; he was also a friend and associate of **Conon of Samos** (<http://www.reunion.iufm.fr/recherche/irem/histoire/conon_de_samos.htm>). His output was prodigious, both in quantity and in quality; and his enquiring mind explored many different fields: geometry, mirrors and lenses, hydraulics, mechanics, architecture, siege craft. His name is inextricably associated with the genesis of engineering in ancient Greece, and with the resolution of many famous mathematical problems. He is perhaps most celebrated, however, for his part in the defense of Syracuse against a besieging Roman fleet. Legend has it that when an act of treachery finally delivered the city to the enemy, a Roman soldier came upon Archimedes working out the answer to a problem in mathematics and killed him on the spot. His burial site was discovered by Cicero in 75 BC" ("Archimedes of Syracuse," *Thessaloniki Science Center & Technology Museum* 2001 <http://www.tmth.edu.gr/en/aet/1/13.html>).

4   **Vacuu-centrific Airship**, 1670 (<http://www.lilienthal-museum.de/olma/home.htm>).

5   "And he came thither unto a **cave**, and lodged there; and behold, the word of the LORD *came* to him, and he said unto him, What doest thou here, Elijah?" I KINGS 19

6   "Have you ever felt like the ministry is **hopeless** and that you might as well die and go to Heaven? That everyone is against you? That perhaps you are ahead of God or behind God or that you should just quit? That no one wants to hear what you have to say? These are the voices to be found in the cave of Elijah! When Elijah came out of the **cave** (wrapped in the prophets mantle) then he was given direction by the Holy Spirit. Elijah was intimidated by the death threat of **Jezebel** (<http://www.seaportsiren.com/>). An intimidated person honors what he fears more than God and thereby submits to what intimidates them. When we are intimidated we transfer our spiritual position of authority to the one intimidating us. The gift of God (the anointing of the Holy Spirit) then lies dormant. We end up furthering the cause of the one intimidating us because we no longer have the power of the Holy Spirit to destroy the yoke of bondage (Isaiah 10:27)" (Hal Warren, "Elijah's Cave, *Faith Cycle Ministries: Helping Christians with Their Next Step in Faith* 2006 <http://www.faithcycleministry.org/HalWarren/SermonOutlines/ElijahsCave.html>).

7   "There's also a legend that a giant **catfish** called *Namazu* lives in mud beneath the Japanese islands. This catfish likes to thrash about; something that could cause untold calamity for the people living above, since this catfish really is *huge*. Fortunately, however, *Namazu* is kept under control by the demigod Kashima. He keeps a huge magical rock in position over the catfish, and as long as Kashima maintains this, people above ground are safe. However, if he relaxes, then people suffer an earthquakes" ("Meaning of the Christian Fish Symbol: Did Christians adopt this sign for their religion from paganism?", *Seiyaku.com* 2004-2006 <http://www.seiyaku.com/customs/fish/fish.html>).

8   For discussion, see: <http://www.americasaves.org/back_page/compound_interest.cfm>.
9   For discussion, see: <http://www.flyfishinghistory.com/contents.htm>.
10   For discussion, see: <http://www.mnsu.edu/emuseum/archaeology/sites/africa/sphinx.html>.
11   For discussion, see: <http://arts.ucsc.edu/faculty/bierman/Elsinore/vengeance/vIllegal.html>.
12   "One of the Hebrew **patriarchs**, mentioned in Genesis 5," (Joseph V. Molloy, "Methusaleh," *New Advent: Catholic Encyclopedia on CD Rom* 2005 <http://www.newadvent.org/cathen/10048b.htm>).
13   For discussion, see: <http://www.visi.com/fall/intro.html>.
14   For discussion, see: <http://www.giulianaconforto.it/English/workshop.htm>.
15   ステンレス アクセサリー ラバー
16   "genus, generis, n.—birth, kind. generate—to produce; to cause to be: *Having generated strong support among the students, the class officers approached the principal with confidence.* Also: generation, regenerate (to cause to be completely renewed; to give a new spiritual life to; to bring into existence again), regeneration, regenerative. [genero, generare, generavi, **generatus**—to beget; to produce]. generative—1) having to do with production; 2) capable of producing: *Noam Chomsky, a professor at M.I.T., attempted through generative grammar (a system of rules that produce all acceptable sentences of a language) to discover "linguistic universals," i.e., deep structures common to all languages.* [*genero*, cf. generate]" (Eugene R. Moutoux, "Latin Derivatives: G," *Latin Derivatives: English Words from Latin for School, Profession, and Everyday Life* 14 November 2001 <http://www.geocities.com/gene_moutoux/pageG.htm>).
17   **Permutation** is not the term that Eliot used. He preferred *intensification* in an attempt to suggest that the foundational substance Generatus, which underlies verisimilitude, remains the same.
18   For discussion, see: <http://www.vitalia-reformhaus.de/>.
19   "In the *Prolegomena*, [Immanuel] Kant introduces a whole new method of doing philosophy, particularly metaphysics, which radically influenced all subsequent philosophy. Kant's paradigm shift is the "**Copernican Turn**," which abandons study of (unknowable) reality-in-itself in favor of inquiry into the world-of-appearances and the innate structures of the mind that determine the nature of experience . . . Kant calls his paradigm shift the "Copernican Turn" because he hopes to accomplish, in metaphysics, the same sort of shift in perspective that Copernicus accomplished in astronomy" (Diana Mertz Hsieh, "Kant's Copernican Turn," *Enlightenment* 8 February 1995 <http://enlightenment.supersaturated.com/essays/text/dianamertzhsieh/kant_turn.html>).
20   "That which is above is from that which is below, and that which is below is from that which is above, working the miracles of one." **Hermes Trismegistus**, trans. Jabir ibn Hayyan (Geber, "Father of Modern Chemistry." For discussion, see: <http://www.nlm.nih.gov/hmd/arabic/bioJ.html.>)
21   For discussion, see: <http://abyss.uoregon.edu/~js/glossary/plato.html>.
22   For discussion, see: <http://www.wf-f.org/Assumption.html>.
23   For discussion, see: <http://plato.stanford.edu/entries/stoicism/>.

THE FAIRIES
By Ludwig Tieck

Johann Ludwig Tieck *(May 31, 1773-April 28, 1853; born in Berlin): poet, translator, editor, novelist, playwright, and critic. The Fairies (Die Elfen) appeared in a three-volume collection of stories and dramas entitled Phantasus (1812-1817). Tieck was a member of the group of early romantic writers, poets, and philosophers active in Jena in 1799, among whom were the brothers Friedrich and August Wilhelm Schlegel and the poet Friedrich von Hardenberg (Novalis). Tieck later became known as the "King of the Romantics," a title that acknowledges his important influence on the movement and the extent to which his writings exemplify romantic themes.*

"Where is Marie, our child?" asked the father.

"She's outside playing on the grass with our neighbor's son," the mother replied.

"I hope they don't run off," worried the father. "They're both so reckless."

The mother looked for the children and brought them their evening bread.

"It's hot!" said the young boy, and little girl cast longing glances toward the red cherries.

"Be careful, children," said the mother, "don't wander too far from the house or into the woods. Father and I are going out to the field."

The young boy Andres answered: "Don't worry; we're afraid of the woods. We'll stay right here at the house near other people."

The mother went off and soon came back again with the father. They closed up the house and set off for the fields to see about the workers harvesting the hay. Their house stood on a small, green prospect, enclosed by a graceful picket fence that protected the fruit trees and flower garden. The village began a bit farther down below, and on the other side of the village stood the lord's castle. Martin, Marie's father, had leased this substantial holding from its aristocratic owner, and he lived there contentedly with his wife and only child. Each year he was able to set some money aside, and he entertained the hopeful prospect of becoming affluent as a result of his industrious activity. The soil was rich, and the lord was not overbearing in his demands.

As he traversed his fields with his wife, the father looked about joyously and said: "Brigitte, how very different this region appears compared to where we live. It is so green here. The whole village is adorned with heavy-laden fruit trees; the soil is thick with lovely plants and flowers; all the houses are tidy and clean; and the inhabitants are well off. It even strikes me that the forests are more beautiful and the skies a deeper blue. As far as the eye can see, one beholds only the joy and pleasure of bountiful nature."

"But as soon as you merely cross to the other side of the stream," said Brigitte, "you find yourself in a completely different landscape. Everything is sad and scrawny. Every traveler agrees that our village is by far and away the most beautiful in the region."

"Yes, right up to the edge of the pine trees," replied her husband. "Take a look back there—how sad and foreboding that secluded plot appears in contrast to the surrounding region. And see behind those dark pines—the sooty huts, the broken-down corrals, the melancholy, overflowing stream."

"That's true," said the wife, as both came to a halt. "A sad, anxious feeling overcomes you near that spot. One hardly knows why. Who can say what sort of people live there—or why they choose to keep so much to themselves, as though they were troubled by bad conscience."

"Poor riff-raff, no doubt," agreed the husband. "They strike me as gypsies, the types who lurk about to rob and cheat honest folk. That's where they have their hideout. I'm amazed that our gracious lord tolerates them."

The wife softened a bit. "Maybe they're poor folk who've fallen on hard times and are ashamed of their poverty. We perhaps shouldn't judge too harshly, although it's certainly odd that they don't show up in church. No one knows how they make ends meet. That tiny, pitiful-looking garden can't nourish them very well—they have no crops to speak of."

"God only knows how they survive," continued the husband, as they again began to walk. "Not a single living soul visits them, because that spot where they squat is cursed and hexed—even the worst ragamuffins keep their distance."

Thus the conversation continued between them as they trod across the fields. The sinister region that held their attention lay on the far side of the village. At a dip in the landscape surrounded by pines, a few huts and various dilapidated farm buildings were visible. Smoke rarely rose from those chimneys. Just as rare, or more so, were the people. Once in blue moon some curious villager, who dared sneak close, caught sight of a detestable hag in a tattered dress. Equally detestable and squalid-looking brats clung to the hag's apron strings. Black dogs led the sad procession. In times of darkness, a brutish knave, whom no one recognized, sauntered over a board that spanned the stream and disappeared into the huts. Then through the gloom one could observe vague, shadowy shapes that wove to and fro, silhouetted by flames. Seen against the tidy houses of the village and the fresh magnificence of the castle, this plot of pines and ruined cottages marred the friendly countenance of the landscape like a scar.

The two children Marie and Andres, having gobbled up their food, decided to have a race. The pert and agile Marie always gave the advantage of an early start to the slower Andres.

"That's no contest!" he finally complained. "Let's try it again, and this time farther. We'll see who wins!"

"Sure," said the girl. "But not across the stream—we're not allowed."

"No," said Andres. "But there's a big pear tree over on that hill—about fifteen minutes from here. I'll run left around the pines—you go right across the field. Once we reach the top, we'll see who's fastest!"

"Fine," said Marie, "that way we won't bump into each other racing. Father said it's all the same to the top, whether you go this side or that side past the gypsies." And she immediately dashed off.

Andres was gone like a shot, and Marie, who turned to the right, didn't see him again.

"He's really stupid," she said to herself. "I only need to screw up my courage, dash across those planks past those huts and through the courtyard and I'll be the first one to the finish."

She came to a halt at the stream in front of the pines.

"Shall I?" she considered. "Oh no! It's just too scary!"

A small, white mutt stood on the far side of the stream and barked as though fit to be tied. Her fear made the beast seem like a monster, and she sprang back.

"O drat!" she said, "that bratty Andres has the lead while I stand here deciding what to do."

The dog barked incessantly, but as she surveyed it more closely it no longer seemed so frightening. On the contrary, it now appeared cute. It had a red collar adorned with bells. Its head shook as it bellowed, and the little bells tinkled merrily.

"Gosh, where's my courage?" swore Marie. "I'll run as fast as I can—and quick before you know it I'll be across and gone. That pooch is not going to chew on me!"

With suchlike thoughts the bold, perky child sprang on to the planks and quickly cleared the distance to the dog, which fell silent and wagged its tail. Now, all of a sudden, she stood in the midst of that place, surrounded by dark pine trees that prevented even a glimpse of her parents' house or the surrounding landscape.

How it all amazed her! She found herself ensconced in the most colorful, festive flower garden filled with vibrant tulips, roses, and lilies. Blue and golden-red butterflies fluttered from blossom to blossom. Exotically colorful birds warbled and sang inside cages hung from glistening wires on a trellis, and golden-haired, bright-eyed children in short, white smocks gamboled about. Some of these played with lambs; others fed the birds or collected flowery bouquets that they gave to each other; still others ate cherries, grapes, and ripened apricots. No huts were to be seen. There stood instead in the middle of that environment a large, beautiful house with an iron door, artfully wrought and decorated. Marie was beside herself with astonishment and could scarcely find her wits. Never one to stand about, however, she straight-away approached the nearest child and took its hand in greeting.

"Have you really come to visit us?" said the lovely child. "I've seen you running and leaping about on the other side. Our dog gave you a fright."

"So you're not really gypsies or scoundrels as everyone says," said Marie. "Those gossips are really stupid."

"Please stay with us," said the marvelous child. "You will like it."

"But I was challenged to a race."

"You'll get back soon enough. Here, have something to eat."

Marie took a taste, and she found the fruit quite sweet—sweeter than any she had ever tasted. Andres, the race, and the warnings of her parents were in a moment completely forgotten.

A large woman in a splendid dress came toward them and questioned Marie.

"Dearest Lady," said Marie, "I ran in here from the outside. With your permission, I'd like to stay."

"Zerina," said the beautiful woman, "you know quite well that she's only allotted a short time here, else you really should have asked for my permission."

"Since she already crossed the bridge, I thought it was all right for her to be here," said the lovely child, "especially since we've often seen her playing in the fields and you yourself have often smiled at her liveliness. She'll leave us soon enough."

"No, I want to stay here!" said Marie. "Here everything is beautiful—and not only that, you have the best toys, and even strawberries and cherries. The outside's nowhere near as nice."

The golden-robed woman stepped back and smiled. Several of the children now sprang forward with smiles and laughter, and they surrounded the happy Marie. They teased her and emboldened her to dance. Some brought her lambs or wonderful toys, while others played music and sang. But Marie felt drawn most strongly to the young playmate that first had greeted her, for this child had the sweetest and friendliest nature of them all.

All at once the little Marie said to the girl: "I'll always stay with you—you'll be my sister!"

Upon hearing this, all the children laughed and joined hands.

"Now let's play a splendid game!" said Zerina.

She quickly ran into the palace and returned with a golden box that contained beautiful clumps of pollen. She took a pinch with her finger and scattered the pollen on the grass. At once the grass began to sway as though stirred by wind, and after a few moments lovely rose bushes sprang up. They quickly grew large and just as quickly unfolded their blossoms, which filled the air with the sweetest scents. Marie took a pinch of pollen, too. As soon as she had scattered it, white lilies and gay daffodils sprang up. Zerina made a quick gesture, and the flowers disappeared, only to be replaced by others a moment later.

"Now," said Zerina, "get ready for something grand."

She stuck two pinecones in the earth and stamped them down heartily. Two green branches appeared.

"Hold on," said Zerina, and Marie looped her arm around the girl's delicate body.

She felt herself lifted upwards as the trees grew with amazing swiftness. The tall pines increased in size, and the two children clung to each other and kissed as the branches swayed in the red clouds of the sunset. The other children clambered up the trees with agile leaps, and they teased and tickled each other amid loud peals of laughter. If by chance one of the children tumbled off a limb, the child flew through the air and settled slowly down to earth unharmed. By and by Marie became alarmed. At this point, the others sang a few loud notes and the trees began to diminish and to return them to the earth after their visit to the clouds.

"Come," said Zerina.

They went through the iron door of the palace. Inside were several beautiful women, old and young, who sat in a circular hall. They nibbled the most exquisite fruits, while strains of lovely melodies, played by invisible musicians, delighted their ears. In the vaulting of the chamber's ceiling, palms, flowers, and greenery had been painted; between this foliage, posed charmingly in playful motion, were the colorful figures of various children. As the music played, this painted scene changed and metamorphosed, all the while glowing with the most intense hues—now green, now blue, now flaming purple—that kindled to a golden sheen. The naked cherubs in the foliage seemed alive, breathing in and out with ruby-red lips, allowing one to catch a glimpse of pearl-white teeth and sparkling, heavenly blue eyes.

Iron steps led downward to a vast, underground room filled with gold, silver, and jewels of varied colors that sparkled brightly between the metal. Wonderful vessels—each apparently filled to the brim with rarities—stood against the walls. The gold had been wrought in the most artful fashion into a variety of forms, and it shimmered gaily. Many small dwarves busied themselves sorting through the treasure and storing it up in the vessels; others—stooped and knock-kneed, with long red noses—lugged about heavy sacks on their sagging shoulders like millers hauling grain. They wheezed and gasped as they broadcast the golden kernels hither and yon. Then they lurched awkwardly right and left and seized at the rolling balls that threatened to roll off course. Not infrequently, one or the other was knocked head over heels into the midst of this hurly burly and smacked the ground like a sack of wheat. They screwed up their faces unpleasantly when Marie laughed at their grotesque shapes and antics.

Behind them sat a little old man with sunken features. Marie greeted him politely, and he thanked her with an earnest nod. He held a scepter and wore a crown. All the other dwarves appeared to acknowledge his authority.

"What's happening here?" he demanded crossly as the children came a bit closer.

Marie kept silent from anxiety, but her companion answered that they'd only entered the room to have a look around.

"Always the same old pranks," said the old one. "Will such idle laziness never end?"

At that he turned his attention to business and resumed his assessment of the gold. He dismissed some of the dwarves and shouted angrily at others.

"Who is that?" asked Marie.

"He is our King of Metals," said the little one, Marie's companion, as they set forth again.

Once more, it seemed they were outside, because they stood next to a large pond, although no sun was shining and up above them they did not see any sky. They entered a small rowboat, and Zerina began to row very energetically. The journey went quickly. As they reached the middle of the pond, Marie saw that a thousand pipes, canals, and streams flowed from there in all directions.

"This water to the right," said the splendid child, "flows down under your garden, which accounts for why everything blooms so freshly. From here you arrive at a great underground river."

Suddenly from the canals and pond, a multitude of children emerged swimming through the water. Many wore wreaths of cattails and water lilies; others held red spikes of coral, and others blew upon conch shells. A wild cacophony resounded gaily from the darkened shores. In and out between the water-babes swan the most beautiful women, and often the young ones jumped from one to the other and clung to their necks with kisses. They all greeted the strangers.

In the midst of this turmoil, the children traveled from the pond into a small river, which became ever narrower. At last the tiny boat came to a halt. The others took their leave, and Zerina banged upon the cliff face. The stones opened like a door, and a large, red womanly being helped them disembark.

"Are things going well?" asked Zerina.

"They are always busy," came the answer, "and so joyful, as you can see. But the temperature is also quite pleasing."

They climbed up a winding staircase, and suddenly Marie found herself in a brilliantly lit salon, so brightly lit that her eyes at first were blinded. Fire-red carpets covered the walls with a purple glow, and as their eyes became more accustomed they saw to their astonishment that human figures appeared to be dancing joyfully to and fro in the patterns of the carpet. These figures were so beautifully proportioned and finely made that one could not imagine anything more charming. Their bodies were of red crystal, so that it seemed that their blood circulated and pulsed visibly. They greeted the new child with laughter and a variety of gestures, but when Marie wanted to go closer Zerina suddenly seized her forcefully and held her back.

"Marie, be careful! It's all fire! It will burn you up!"

Marie felt the heat.

"Why don't those darling creatures come out and play?"

"Just as you live in air, they must live in fire. They'd perish outside it. See how it suits them, how they laugh and take delight. Those there on the bottom disperse the streams of fire toward every corner of the underworld, and from those streams grow the flowers, fruits, and wine. The red currents flow alongside streams; those beings of flame are always active and joyful. But come, let's return to the outer garden. It's too hot for you here."

Outside, the scene had changed. Moonlight lay upon all the flowers; the birds were silent, and the children slept in varied groups amid the arbor. Marie and her friend, however, did not feel tired. On the contrary, they wandered in happy conversation throughout the warm summer night until it was morning.

As day broke, they breakfasted on fruits and milk. Marie said: "Let's go out to the pine trees, just for the fun of it, to see how they look."

"Good," said Zerina, "and while we're there you can visit our sentinels, who will certainly please you. They're standing on the ramparts between the trees."

They went through the flower garden, through graceful groves filled with the melodies of nightingales, climbed over vine-laden hills, and after following the windings of a clear-running stream, they came at last to the pine trees on the rise that marked the border of that domain.

"How is it that we've covered so great a distance when from the outside this place appears so small?" asked Marie.

"I don't know," answered her friend. "It's simply that way."

They climbed to the dark pine trees, and a cold wind blew upon them from the outer world. A foggy mist lay upon the surrounding landscape. Above perched marvelous shapes and figures with white-dusted faces; they were not unlike the disagreeable white heads of owls. The figures wore folded cloaks of ragged wool, and they held open umbrellas over their remarkable heads. They swayed and bobbed unceasingly with bats that winged adventurously from the rock.

"I'd like to laugh, yet I'm afraid," said Marie.

"Those are our good and vigilant sentinels," said Marie's small companion. "They stand here and create wind, so that anyone who dares to approach will see them and experience paralyzing fear and sublime terror. Right now they are under wraps, because outside it is cold and rainy, which is weather they cannot abide. Snow and wind never touch us here below—nor even a cold breeze. Here it is eternal summer and spring. If those above didn't frequently change their shifts, they would die.

"Who are you?" asked Marie, as she again descended into the scent of flowers. "Or are you nameless?"

"We're called Fairies," said the friendly child. "I've heard that we're much talked about in the world."

They heard a great commotion in the meadow.

"The beautiful bird has arrived!" shouted the children. Everyone hurried into the hall. The two peered inside, as young and old shoved to get in. Everyone cheered, while from within sounded jubilant music.

As soon as they were inside, they saw that the circular space was filled with all manner of shapes and figures. They all gazed upward at a giant bird whose brilliant plumage described circles above them in the dome as it flew back and forth. The music sounded more joyous than ever, and the colors and lights pulsed faster.

At last the music stilled and the bird fluttered with a sweeping whoosh down to a sparkling crown, which hovered under the high windows and was illuminated from the vaulting. Its feathers were purple and green, streaked with brilliant, golden stripes. On its head, blazing like jewels, swayed a feathery diadem. The bird's beak was red and its legs bright blue. As it settled down, all the colors of its feathers shimmered together, enchanting the eye.

The bird was the size of an eagle. But when it opened its beak, a sweet melody rose from its heaving breast in tones as charming as a nightingale's. It sang the song strongly into the chamber like beams of light, so that everyone down to the smallest child wept with enchantment and rapture. Once the song ended, everyone bowed. The bird then flew in circles throughout the dome, swooped through the door, and ascended into bright sky, where it soon shone no more vividly than a dying ember and at last was lost to sight.

"Why are you all so happy?" asked Marie, and she inclined herself toward a beautiful child, who seemed smaller than the day before.

"The King is coming," said the little one. "Many of us have not yet seen him. Wherever he goes, good luck and gaiety follow. For quite a while, we've longed for him, just as you long for spring after a tedious winter. And now the bird, his lovely ambassador, has announced the King's arrival. That admirable and judicious bird that comes to us in the service of the King is called Phoenix. He lives far away in Arabia atop a tree—the only one like it in the world—just as the Phoenix is the only bird of its kind in the world. When Phoenix feels old, he weaves a nest out of balsam and frankincense, sets it on fire, and burns up alive. He dies singing, and out of the drifting ashes a rejuvenated Phoenix is reborn.

The Phoenix seldom takes flight; people see him only once in a century or so, but whenever they catch sight of him they record the encounter in their chronicles and mark the event as a harbinger of miraculous times. But now, my dear friend, you must depart, for the countenance of the King is not inclined toward you."

The lovely woman, clad in gold, strolled through the throng, gestured Marie to follow, and went with her to a lonely pathway in the arbor.

"Dear child, you must leave us," she said. "The King will hold court here for twenty years, maybe longer. Blessings and fertility will spread throughout the land, but most of all in the regions bordering. All fountains and streams will flow more abundantly; fields and gardens will bear more richly; the wine will sweeten; the meadow flower, the wood grow fresh and green; mild breezes will blow, foul weather vanish, and no bank will overflow. Take this ring, think of us later. Yet, beware what you say to those with whom you share these memories, or else we will be forced to flee this country. All who live here, including you, share in the luck and blessings of our presence. Now, for one last time, kiss your darling playmate farewell."

She left, and Zerina wept. Marie bent down to embrace her, and they parted.

Already she stood on the rickety bridge. A cold wind blew through pine trees. The small dog barked and howled; its bells tinkled. She looked back, then hurried away—seized by an anxious tremor at the sight of those dark pine trees, ruined cottages, and deepening shadows.

"How worried my parents must be!" she said to herself, as she reached the field. "And I can't even tell them what happened. Even if I did, they wouldn't believe me!"

Two men went by, and she greeted them. As they passed, she heard one say: "That's a pretty girl. Is she from around here?"

With nervous footsteps, she hurried on to her parent's house, but the trees that stood full of fruit just yesterday now stood barren and leafless. The house had been repainted, and she saw a new barn nearby.

Marie stood in wonderment. She thought she was dreaming. Confused, she opened the door. Behind the dinner table sat her father. He sat between two strangers: a woman and a boy.

"My god, Father!" she cried. "Where's Mother?"

"Mother?" said the woman, in a trembling tone of voice. She stood up. "No, it can't be—is it true? You! The lost child! We thought you were dead. It's you—our little Marie!"

She could recognize Marie at once. She knew her from the small, brown mole under the child's chin, and by her eyes and shape.

They all embraced joyfully. The adults wept with happiness. Marie was amazed that she stood almost as tall as her father. She could not understand why her mother looked so different and older. She asked about the boy.

"He's our neighbor's son, Andres," said her father, Martin. "Marie, how is it you're so suddenly returned to us after seven long years? Where have you been? Why haven't we heard a single word of you in all this time?"

"Seven years?" said Marie. She could not make sense of it. "Seven whole years?"

"Yes!" said Andres, laughing. He squeezed her hand lovingly. "I won the race, Marie! I've been to the pear tree and back for seven years—and you, you slow poke, you only just got here!"

They asked her many questions and demanded explanations, but because of her oath to Zerina, she could not answer. Seeing her so dumb, they invented an explanation for themselves: she must have lost her way, hitched a ride on a passing farm cart, and found her way at last to a strange locale where no one knew her or her parents. Those strangers had taken her to a far distant city where some good people raised and fostered her. After a time, when her foster parents died, the desire arose in her to find the place where she had been born. And thus, when an opportunity to travel came her way, she seized it and came home.

"All's well that ends well," said the mother. "Enough! Thank heavens you've returned, my one and only!"

Andres stayed for supper, but Marie felt completely lost. The house felt cramped and dark. She felt amazed by their manner of dress, which, though simple and clean, felt alien. She noticed the ring on her finger, in which sat a flaming red gem amid marvelous, gleaming gold. In answer to her father's question, she replied that the ring was a gift from her benefactor.

She felt glad when the time to sleep came at last, and she hurried to bed.

The next morning she felt more like herself. The world made better sense. It was easier to answer the questions put to her by villagers who stopped by to say hello.

Andres was one of the earliest to come—eager and happy to see her. He'd spent a sleepless night thinking about her, charmed by the change that the years had made in her appearance.

The townsfolk demanded that she tell her tale at the castle. Soon she had done so. The aging lord and his gracious lady heard her with amazement. Marie's speech and appearance were honest, and she answered their questions in a frank, straightforward way. She had lost her fear for highborn folk—compared to the wonder and splendor of the fairies, the castle and its inhabitants seemed dull and earthy. The world held these people in its grasp.

All the young men felt charmed by her beauty.

February came.

The trees blossomed earlier than usual; the nightingale had never sung so early. Spring outpaced itself with beauty, turning the landscape green far sooner than the oldest gray beard could recall. Streams irrigated every corner of the land, and the meadows and fields drank deep. The hills seemed higher; the vineyards thicker; the fruit trees blossomed dense as never before. A mild, soft-swelling blessing wafted across the landscape like a sweet-scented cloud. Everything swelled to harvest beyond expectation—no harsh weather, no storm to damage the fruit. The grapes swelled heavy on the vines, and the inhabitants of that landscape were astounded—they felt ensconced by the sweetest of dreams.

The next year was the same, though people were more accustomed to the extraordinary.

In autumn, Marie acceded to the Andres' heartfelt pleas; she agreed to be his bride, and in winter they were wed.

Often with longing Marie recalled her sojourn behind the pine trees. Her mood remained earnest and withdrawn. As lovely as it was all about her, she could still recall something even lovelier—and the quiet sadness of this memory inclined her to melancholy. It pained her to hear her father or husband talk about the gypsies and vagabonds who lived in the forest hollow. She often wanted to tell them how she had enjoyed those strangers' hospitality—especially Andres, who appeared to delight in her parents' criticisms—but she held back. Thus her year passed by, and in the next year she gave birth to a daughter, whom she named Faye, to remind her of the fairies.

The young people lived together with father Martin and mother Brigitte, for the house was ample enough for everyone. They helped the parents with work on their extensive farm.

Little Faye soon demonstrated strange talents and abilities. She ran extremely fast and could talk when she was no more than one-year old. After only a few years, her precocious nature and startling beauty astonished everyone. Her mother could not hold back the thought that her daughter looked remarkably like the lovely children in the pine hollow.

Faye didn't mix with other children. She avoided them and their noisy games; she preferred to be alone. Often she withdrew to a corner of the garden, where she read or worked diligently at some task. Persons often caught her drawn deeply into herself, or sometimes saw her energetically walking back and forth, conversing with no one. The two parents left her alone—she seemed fit enough and healthy—but they noted with care her unusual precocious speech and behavior.

"A wise child like that will not grow old," said her grandmother Brigitte often. "She's too good for this world. She'll never feel at home here."

The little one had the peculiar quality of wanting to do everything by herself; she would not let anyone help her. She was almost always the first one up in the morning; she washed herself carefully and got dressed alone. She was just as fastidious in the evening, taking care to fold and put away her clothing and wash herself. She allowed no one, not even her mother, to fuss with her possessions. Her mother made allowances for this behavior and thought no more of it, but she was surprised on one of the festival days when she had to dress Faye against her will for a visit to the castle. The little one protested with shrieks and tears, and in the midst of her distress, her mother Marie saw a remarkable gold coin hanging from the young one's neck upon a thread. Marie at once recognized it, for it resembled those she had seen once upon a time in the realm of fairy.

The little one was dismayed, and she confessed finally that she had found the coin in the garden. It pleased her, so she had kept it and guarded it carefully. Now she pleaded for it so passionately and with such heartfelt sincerity that Marie placed it back about her neck. Child in hand and thoughtful and reflective, the mother wended her way to the castle.

On the side of the family farmhouse stood some buildings used to store fruits and tools, and behind these grew a grassy patch amid an old grove of trees. No one visited this place. The newly built storage buildings put the grove at an awkward distance from the garden.

Faye loved to linger in this quiet, out-of-the-way place. No one bothered to disturb her here, and sometimes her parents lost sight of her for half-a-day or longer.

One afternoon the mother went to clean these storage buildings and to look for something she had misplaced. While she puttered about, a beam of light shone through a chink in the wall. Seeing it, Marie had an impulse to peep outside to see what her daughter might be doing. She moved aside a loose stone in order to spy more clearly into the grove.

Faye sat within the grove on a little bench. Beside her sat someone Marie knew very well: Zerina.

The two children played together and took delight in each other's company in the most harmonious way. The fairy child embraced her beautiful playmate and said sadly: "Ah, you darling creature. I once played this way with your mother, once upon a time when she was young and came to visit us. But you mortals age too quickly; before you know it, you're grown and reasonable. That's such a shame. If only you could remain young like me!"

"I'd gladly do it to make you happy," said Faye. "But you mean everyone. I'll soon be grown and reasonable and no longer interested in games, for everyone tells me I'm advanced for my age. Ah! And then I won't see you any more, dear little Zerina! It'll all be over and done with—just like with blossoms. How splendid is the blossoming apple tree with its red swelling buds. The tree grows so large and broad that everyone who passes beneath it marvels and feels that it is becoming something special. Then the sun comes along; blossom becomes fruit; and soon enough the hard kernel inside the fruit shoulders aside all this colorful gaiety. He knocks it down—he can't do anything else. As summer swings to autumn, the tree must fruit. True, an apple is a lovely thing, but such a thing's nothing compared to spring blossoms. It's the same way with mortals. I don't look forward to growing old. Oh, if only I could visit you one more time!"

"Ever since the King came to dwell with us, such things have become impossible," said Zerina. "Listen, I'll visit you as often as I can, my darling. No one sees me; no one knows about this—not in your world, not in mine. I pass through the air invisibly, or fly here like a bird. We'll still have many days together, as long as you're young. Now what can I do to make you happy?"

"Love me just as much as I love you! Come, let's make a rose together."

Zerina took a tiny box from her dress, threw two seeds inside, and suddenly there stood a green rose bush in front of them with two blood-red roses. The two roses inclined toward each other as though kissing.

Laughing with delight, the children plucked the roses, and the bush immediately disappeared.

"Must the rose also die so quickly!" said Faye. "Red child, wonder of the earth!"

"Give it here," said the tiny fairy. She breathed upon the rose three times and kissed it lovingly. Handing it back, she said: "Now it will remain fresh and in blossom until winter."

"I'll guard it as though it were a portrait of you," said Faye. "Each morning and evening I'll take it out from its place of hiding and kiss it—just as if it were you."

"The sun's going down," said Zerina. "I must go home."

They embraced for one last time, and then Zerina was gone.

That evening, Marie embraced her child with a feeling of anxiety and trepidation. She allowed the lovely girl more freedom than ever before, and she often assuaged her husband's feeling of anger when he came looking for her, which he did from time to time. He did not like the way Faye shied from other people, and he worried that this excessive solitude might turn her into a simpleton.

The mother often crept secretly to the chink in the wall. Almost every time she did so, she saw the marvelous fairy child keeping company with Faye. The two sat together in games or intimate conversation.

"Would you like to fly?" Zerina once asked her friend.

"Oh yes!"

At once the fairy creature took hold of the mortal and rose with her from the ground. They ascended to the tops of the trees.

The worried mother forgot her caution; terrified, she craned her head above the wall to see them better.

Zerina noticed her. Smiling, she raised her finger in a gesture of caution, settled back to earth with the child, gave Faye a hug, and disappeared.

From now on, the marvelous fairy spotted Marie more and more often, and each time the fairy shook her finger or head, although with a friendly gesture.

Often after an argument with her husband, Marie said to him heatedly: "You're unfair to those poor people who live in the pine cottages!"

When Andres then demanded to know why she felt that her opinion of the matter held more weight than the combined judgments of the villagers and the lord of their estate, Marie broke off and fell silent.

One day Andres became even more heated than usual in declaring that homeless riff-raff should be persecuted and driven from the countryside. At this, Marie could not restrain herself: "Be quiet! They are our benefactors!"

"Benefactors?" said Andres, surprised. "Those worthless vagrants?"

Overcome with anger, Marie made the mistake of telling him the story from her childhood after making him promise never to tell a soul. Seeing him shake his head in doubt and disbelief as she confessed, Marie took his hand and led him to the place near the grove where Andres espied to his astonishment the two snuggling playmates: fairy and child.

He did not know what to say. A cry of astonishment escaped him, and Zerina looked up. She suddenly trembled and became pale. Angry and without any hint of friendship, she made a threatening gesture and said to Faye: "It's not your fault, my dear one, but you will never be wise, no matter how smart you may appear to be."

She embraced the little one with stormy haste, and then, with a shrill cry, and in the shape of crow, she flew away toward the pine trees.

That evening the little one was very quiet. She wept and kissed the rose that Zerina had given her. Marie was beside herself with anxiety. Andres said little.

Night came.

Suddenly, the trees outside began to rustle. Birds flew nervously here and there with frightened cries. It thundered; the earth trembled; and a cry of lamentation filled the air. Marie and Andres were too frightened to stand. They covered themselves with blankets and awaited the coming of day with fear and trembling. Toward morning the tumult lessened as the sun rose over the wood.

Andres got dressed, and as he did Marie noticed that the stone on the ring that he wore had turned pale. When she opened the door, the clear sunlight streamed toward her, but she hardly could recognize the landscape that she beheld. The freshness of the forest had vanished; the hills looked sunken; the streams flowed in a trickle; the sky was gray—and the pine trees (the ones that grew in the direction of the cottages) now looked no more dismal than any other tree. And the cottages behind the pines were not in any way threatening at all.

Quite a few villagers came to swap tales of the unusual night events. They told how they had gone to the place where the gypsies had settled—and they told how those folk must have fled, for now their huts stood empty. Instead of gypsies, the townsfolk had found inside the dwellings ordinary, everyday poor people like themselves. A few odd pieces of furniture had been left behind.

Faye said to her mother secretly: "Last night, in the howling fury, when I couldn't sleep and lay with my hands clasped in prayer, my door suddenly sprang open and my fairy playmate entered to say farewell. She had a traveling bag beside her, a hat on her head, and large hiking staff in her hand. She was very cross and angry at you. Because of you, she now faced the most painful punishments—all because she had loved you so very much. She told me that everyone departed this region with aching regret."

Marie forbade her to tell this to anyone else.

Among those arriving, came the ferryman across the river, and he, too, had marvelous tales to tell.

He related how on the eve of that terrible night a large stranger came to him and had rented the ferry for use from sunset until dawn. The stranger had made one demand: "Remain inside your house. Lie still and asleep in bed. Do not venture outdoors, even for the least curiosity."

"I was terrified," said the old ferryman. "But the awful uproar did not allow me to sleep. I crept to the window and peered out toward the river. Tremendous clouds scudded angrily across the heavens, and the distant trees thrashed about. It felt as though my tiny house would quake and shake to pieces. Suddenly I saw a stream of white light that became stronger and brighter—bright as a thousand fallen stars. It shimmered and played about the darkened pine trees, flowed over the fields, and broadened toward the river. Then I heard a whirring, scurrying, hurrying, rustling noise, closer and closer. It moved toward my boat. Into that ferry climbed all manner of shining creatures—large and small, male and female—and children, too, as it appeared. The stranger ferried them all. They crossed the river, and in the waves, next to the ferryboat, swam and fluttered a thousand brilliant shapes. The mist streamed with fluttering lights. The entire company howled and complained that they were forced to leave their accustomed homeland to travel into exile to some far distant place. The rudder fought the wake, and then the weather suddenly quieted. Back and forth went the ferryboat, each time laden with new travelers. They took many pots and containers with them; the most hideous little monsters lugged them aboard—goblins or devils, I'm not sure. Amid this brilliance came a grand procession. I thought I could espy a gray-haired elder at its head. He rode a small, white stallion, and everyone pressed toward him. I could see only the head of the horse—it was bedecked with a costly and brilliant livery—and on the patriarch's head sat a crown. He made such a splendid impression that I thought that the sun had risen as he crossed the raging stream. Thus the events unfolded the entire night. At last I slept like a man who has lost his senses, battered by joy and terror. Come morning, all was still, although the river ran so high and wild I had trouble steering my boat to make the crossing."

That same year saw births that were stunted and malformed. The woods sickened and died. The fountains ran dry. That region, which travelers once had crossed with such delight, stood barren in autumn—naked and cold. There was scarcely a plot of ground in that extremity of sand where the least green sprout could be noticed. The fruit trees withered; the vineyards dried. The landscape made such a tragic impression that in the following year the lord and his family deserted the castle, which by and by collapsed into ruin.

Day and night, Faye guarded her rose and thought of her fairy playmate with tender longing. Just as the flowers fade and wilt, so, too, did she. Long before the next spring came round, the child had died.

Marie often stood weeping on that plot of ground before the little hut, and there she mourned her departed blessings. She pined away just like her child, and in a few short years she followed Faye to the grave.

And old father Martin moved back to his former home in the company of his stepson.